*youth without youth*

*with a new foreword by*
**FRANCIS FORD COPPOLA**

**youth**

MIRCEA ELIADE

# *without youth*

the university of chicago press
chicago and london

MIRCEA ELIADE was born in 1907 in Bucharest, Romania. He studied philosophy and religion in Bucharest and Calcutta and became an influential historian of religions and Eastern philosophy. He taught first at the Sorbonne and then at the University of Chicago until his death in 1986. Eliade published over 1,300 works of scholarship and fiction, including the three-volume *History of Religious Ideas*, several autobiographical novels, and three volumes of short stories.

The University of Chicago Press, Chicago 60637
The University of Chicago Press, Ltd., London
© Éditions Gallimard, 1981
Translation © 1988 by Mac Linscott Ricketts
Foreword © 2007 by Francis Ford Coppola.
Translation from Romanian of *Tinereţi fără de Tinereţi*. First published in *Revista scriitorilor români* (Munich) no. 15 (1978): 49–82 and no. 16 (1979): 33–73
Originally published in French as *Le Temps d'un centenaire* (c) Éditions Gallimard, 1982
First published in the United States by Ohio State University Press, 1988
The University of Chicago Press edition, 2007
Printed in the United States of America
16 15 14 13 12 11 10 09 08 07     1 2 3 4 5
ISBN-13: 978-0-226-20415-4 (paper)
ISBN-10: 0-226-20415-4 (paper)

Library of Congress Cataloging-in-Publication Data
Eliade, Mircea, 1907–1986.
  [Tinerete fără de tinerete. English]
  Youth without youth / Mircea Eliade ; translated by Mac Linscott Ricketts.
    p. cm.
  ISBN-13: 978-0-226-20415-4 (pbk. : alk. paper)
  ISBN-10: 0-226-20415-4 (pbk. : alk. paper)
  I. Ricketts, Mac Linscott. II. Title.
  PC839.E38T5613 2007
  859'.334—dc22                    2006038079

⊚ The paper used in this publication meets the minimum requirements of the American National Standard for Information Sciences—Permanence of Paper for Printed Library Materials, ANSI Z39.48-1992.

# *foreword*

BY FRANCIS FORD COPPOLA

*Youth Without Youth:* A World War II–era film about an elderly professor whose mysterious rejuvenation makes him a target for the Nazis, it is a love story wrapped in a mystery.

That's how I think of the film, having seen it only a few days ago. But perhaps it would be more interesting to go back to when I was reading the story by Mircea Eliade for the first time and became inspired to make a film of it.

*"What do we do with time? . . . Time, the supreme ambiguity of the human condition."* MIRCEA ELIADE

The subject matter of any film you choose to make is doubly important because the process of filmmaking is such a relentless, tedious, and difficult experience that you have to be sure the theme is something that will sustain your interest. No matter how tough things get, or how discouraged you may feel, you have to be sure that morning after morning you'll wake up to a subject that still fascinates you. It should preferably be a subject you don't quite understand, even better if it's based on a question you don't know the answer to. Then the making of the film, which ultimately winds through several years, can provide an answer, which will be the film itself.

I had spent the last several years laboring over an ambitious original screenplay that was defying my efforts to complete it. The project was intended to be the crowning moment of my career; it was ambitious, with grand themes and scope, and even aspired to contribute new ideas to the present state of cinematic language. I had decided that my film could go further in exploring two areas, Time and Interior Consciousness.

The cinema itself is only one hundred years old, and during that time (especially through the silent era), pioneer filmmakers knew very little about the language of the motion pictures because it didn't yet exist. Things like the "close-up," parallel editing, and montage evolved out of their experimentation. Great silent filmmakers such as

Edwin S. Porter, D. W. Griffith, G. W. Pabst, and Sergei Eisenstein had to invent a language as they went along. As the financiers of the day were more interested in getting the reels into their nickelodeons than in imposing creative controls, the directors were left to their own devices. Later, in our modern era, that experimentation became "frozen" in order to insure profits and reduce loss. But I felt it was naive to think that everything had been discovered, and so I set about to try to further widen the cinematic language, especially in those two areas—the filmic expressions of Time and of Interior Consciousness.

When I showed my ambitious, unfinished screenplay to a high school friend, Wendy Doniger (who as a young girl was not only pretty, but brilliant, and who is now an eminent professor of Oriental studies, a Sanskritist, and holder of the Eliade chair at the University of Chicago), she helpfully sent back notes, including some quotes from the writings of her mentor, Mircea Eliade:

"The question, 'what do we do with Time?' expresses the supreme ambiguity of the human condition. . . . Actually it is not a dream, but it takes part in the illusory nature of dreaming because it is the future, therefore of time. Now, time is par excellence unreal. . . ."

These lines are spoken in the film by the legendary Italian Sanskritist and explorer Professor Giuseppe Tucci, a real-life idol of Eliade's.

I became fascinated with the main character of the story, Dominic Matei—a polymath, linguist, Sanskritist, and expert on the subject of comparative religion, much as Eliade himself was. Put that in the context that at the time, I was a sixty-six-year-old man who had spent years on a screenplay that I was never able to complete to my satisfaction, reading about a man who had become seventy with the fear that he had begun to lose his powers and would never be able to complete his life's work, and who quite amazingly finds himself made young again. And not only put back into the prime of his life, in better physical shape than ever, but like Faust—granted his deepest wish, to have his intellectual abilities greatly enlarged along with his memory and other "powers." Because Eliade was also a passionate linguist indulging in wish-fulfillment, Dominic's ultimate desire was a "deeper understanding of the origins of language." Eliade's story moved with one totally unexpected step after another, taking me with it.

At once I thought, this is what I have been looking for, something to rescue me from the mire my unfinished screenplay had stuck me in—a fable about a man somewhat my age, made young again and given the ability to achieve what he had been working toward his entire life. And to fall in love, "one last time."

I hadn't made a film in almost ten years. As always, as in my youth, I wanted to make personal films, art films, experimental films—all those kinds of films no one would want to finance. I decided I could learn from my daughter Sofia, who went off to Japan and, by working in a youthful guerrilla filmmaking style, made *Lost in Translation* on her own terms. The very thought excited me, that perhaps *I* could also make a film in a "youthful guerrilla style." I was sure I still could. I realized that, like Dominic Matei, I could take for myself the freedom I associated with youth, and along with that a chance to be a young filmmaker once again.

The film would have to be about many things—time, memory, second chances, the illusion of the new man, European history, love and using the one we love, language—and I knew that the only sensible way to deal with this dilemma was to become young again, to forget everything I knew and to try to have the mind of a student. To reinvent myself by forgetting I ever had any film career at all, and instead to dream about having one. So the themes of this film, *Youth Without Youth*, would be the themes of this moment in my own life, something that is a prerequisite to the film "being" what it's about, which is the highest form of cinema.

*youth without youth*

# I

Only when he heard the bell of the Metropolian Church
did he remember that it was the night of Easter. And suddenly the rain seemed unnatural — the rain which had
greeted him as he had emerged from the railway station
and which threatened to become torrential. He made his
way forward hastily with the umbrella brought down to
his shoulders, his eyes downcast, trying to avoid the riv-
ulets. Without realizing it, he began to run, holding the
umbrella close to his chest, like a shield. But after some
twenty meters he saw the traffic signal turn red, and he
had to stop. He waited nervously, standing on tiptoe,
hopping from one foot to the other continually, looking
in consternation at the little pond that covered a good
part of the boulevard directly in front of him. The traffic light changed, and in the next moment he was shaken,
blinded by an explosion of white incandescent light. He
felt as though he had been sucked up by a fiery cyclone
that had exploded at some mysterious moment on top
of his head. A close strike of lightning, he said to himself,
blinking with difficulty to unseal his eyelids. He did not

understand why he was clutching the handle of his umbrella so hard. The rain lashed at him wildly from all sides at once, and yet he felt nothing. Then he heard the bell at the Metropolian again, and all the other bells, and very close by still another, striking in a solitary, desperate way. I've had a fright, he said to himself, and he began to shiver. It's because of the water, he realized a few moments later, becoming aware of the fact that he was lying in the puddle near the curb. I've taken a chill. . . .

"I saw the lightning strike him," he heard the breathless voice of a frightened man saying. "I don't know if he's still alive or not. I was looking over there, where he was standing under the traffic signal, and I saw him light up from head to toe — umbrella, hat, coat, all at once! If it hadn't been for the rain, he would have been burnt to a crisp. I don't know if he's still alive or not."

"And even if he's still alive, what can we do with him?" The voice seemed to come from far away and it sounded to him tired, bitter.

"Who knows what sins he's committed, that God would strike him on the very night of Easter, right behind a church!" Then, after a pause, he added, "Let's see what the intern says about it."

It seemed strange to him that he felt nothing, that he did not, in fact, feel his body at all. He knew from the conversation of those around him that he had been moved. But how had he been transported? In their arms? On a stretcher? On a cart of some sort? . . .

"I don't believe he has a chance," he heard another

voice saying later, also far away. "Not a single centimeter of his skin is untouched. I don't understand how he stays alive. Normally, he would have been . . ."

*Of course, everybody knows that. If you have lost more than fifty percent of your skin, you die of asphyxia.* But he realized quickly that it was ridiculous and humiliating to reply mentally to the people bustling around him. He would have liked not to have had to hear them, just as, with his eyes shut tight, he did not see them. And at the same moment he found himself far away, happy, as he had been *then*.

ༀ ༀ ༀ "And then, what else happened," she asked him in jest, smiling. "What other tragedy?"

"I didn't say it was a tragedy, but in a sense it was that: to conceive a passion for science, to have but one desire—to dedicate your life to science."

"To which science are you referring?" she interrupted him. "To mathematics or to the Chinese language?"

"To both—and to all the others I've discovered and fallen in love with, insofar as I've learned about them."

She put her hand on his arm to keep him from getting angry at being interrupted again. "Mathematics I understand, because if you didn't have a vocation for it, it would be useless to persevere. But *Chinese?*"

He didn't know why he burst into laughter. Probably he was amused by the way she had said, "But *Chinese?*"

"I thought I'd told you. Two years ago in the fall when I was in Paris I went to a lecture by Chavannes. I saw him after class in his office; he asked me how long I'd been studying Chinese and how many other Oriental languages I knew. No need to repeat the whole conversation. I understood just one thing: that if I didn't master in a few years—in a *few years*—Chinese, Sanskrit, Tibetan, and Japanese, I would never become a great orientalist."

"All right, but you must have told him that you wanted to study *only* the Chinese language."

"That's what I said, but I didn't persuade him. Because even in that case I'd still have to learn Japanese and a lot of South Asian languages and dialects. . . . But this wasn't the important thing; it was something else. When I told him I'd been studying Chinese for five months, he stepped to a blackboard and wrote some twenty characters. He asked me to pronounce them one by one, and then to translate the passage. I pronounced them as best I could, and I translated some, but not all, of them. He smiled amiably. 'That's not bad,' he said, 'But if after five months . . . How many hours a day?' 'At least six hours,' I replied. 'Then the Chinese language is not for you. Probably you don't have the necessary visual memory. . . . My dear sir,' he added with a smile that was ambiguous, affectionate, and ironic at the same time, 'My dear sir, in order to master Chinese you must have the memory of a Mandarin, a *photographic memory*. If you don't have it, you will be obliged to make an effort three or four times as great. I don't believe it's worth it.' 'So, basically it's a matter of memory.' 'Of a photographic memory,' he repeated gravely, emphasizing the words." ༓ ༓ ༓

6

He heard the door opening and closing several times and other noises, including strange voices.

"Let's see what the Professor says. If you ask me, I'd say that frankly . . ."

The same thing, over and over again! But he liked the voice; it was, no doubt, that of a young doctor, clever and enthusiastic about his profession, generous.

". . . His skin was burned one hundred percent, and yet he's survived twelve hours, and so far as we can tell, he's not in pain. . . . Have you given him any shots?"

"One, this morning. I thought he groaned. But maybe he was just moaning in his sleep."

"Do you know anything about him? Was anything found beside him?"

"Just the handle of the umbrella. The rest was incinerated. Curious — the handle, of all things, a wooden handle. . . . The clothes were turned to ashes. What the rain didn't wash away was saved in the ambulance."

He knew it would have had to be that way, and yet hearing the intern say it lifted his spirits. So, the two envelopes in his pocket had been incinerated, too. . . .

༓ ༓ ༓ Without intending to, because he had not been careful to close the door completely behind him, he had overheard: "The Old Man's getting quite decrepit! He told us the same thing three or four times."

It was true. He had been impressed by the news he had read in *La Fiera Letteraria*, that Papini was almost blind and no surgeon dared to operate on him. For a ravenous and indefatigable reader like Papini, this was an unparalleled tragedy. That is why he kept talking about it all the time. But perhaps Vaian was right: I *am* beginning to get decrepit.

Then he heard the voice again. "And what other tragedy befell you? You gave up the Chinese language. What else?"

"As a matter of fact, I didn't give it up; I continued to learn ten or fifteen characters per day, but this was mostly for my pleasure and because it helped me to understand the translations of the texts I read. Actually, I was a dilettante."

"So much the better," Laura interrupted him, placing her hand on his arm again. "There have to be a few intelligent men with enough imagination to enjoy the discoveries made by your great scholars. It's a good thing you dropped Chinese. . . . But what are the other tragedies you referred to?"

He looked at her a long time. She was far from being the best-looking female student he had known, but she was *different*. He did not understand what attracted him, why he sought her continually, going through the lecture halls where he had not walked for three or four years, since he had taken his Degree. He knew he would always find her at Titu Maiorescu's class. There he had met her an hour ago, and, as usual, when he escorted her to her home, they had stopped to sit on a bench beside a lake in Cişmigiu.

"What are the other tragedies?" she repeated, maintaining her calm, smiling gaze.

"I told you that while I was still in the lycée, I was fond

of mathematics and music, but I also liked history, archeology, and philosophy. I wanted to study them all; obviously, not as a specialist, but still rigorously, working directly from texts, because I have a horror of improvisation and hearsay learning."

She interrupted him, raising her arms in a boyish gesture.

"You're the most ambitious man I've ever met! The most ambitious and the most driven! Driven, especially!"

⁂

He knew the voices well, and had learned to distinguish them. There were three nurses by day and two at night.

"If he had any luck, he'd die now. Because they say that whoever dies during the Week of Light goes straight to Paradise."

She has a good soul; she pities me. She's better than the others because she's thinking about my salvation. . . . But what if she gets the idea of pulling the I.V. needle out of my vein? Probably I'd survive till morning when the intern comes. And if he doesn't notice it, the Professor will. The Professor is the only one who's in despair and humiliated over the fact that he doesn't understand; the only one who wants at all costs to keep me alive, to find out what happened. He had heard him one day — no use asking *when* — he had heard him talking after he had touched his eyelids with infinite care:

"The eye seems intact, but if he's blind or not, I don't know. I don't know *anything*, in fact. . . ."

He had heard this also: "I don't even know if he's conscious or not, if he hears or if he *understands* what he hears." It wasn't his fault. Several times before that he had recognized the voice and had understood it perfectly. "If you understand what I say," the Professor shouted, "squeeze my finger." But he could not feel his finger. He would have liked to squeeze it, but he didn't know how.

That time the Professor added, "If we can succeed in keeping him alive another five days . . ."

In five days, one of his assistants found out, the great specialist from Paris, Professor Gilbert Bernard, would come to Bucharest en route to Athens.

ঠ ঠ ঠ "Especially, ambitious!" Laura repeated. "You want to be what all those other people are: philologist, orientalist, archeologist, historian, and who knows what else. That is, you want to live a strange life, a different life, instead of being yourself, Dominic Matei, and cultivating your own genius exclusively."

"My genius?" he exclaimed with a pretended modesty in order to hide his delight. "That presupposes I *have* genius!"

"In a sense, certainly, you do have it. You don't resemble anyone I have ever met. You live life and understand it differently from us."

"But up to now, at age twenty-six, I haven't accomplished anything. I've just taken all the exams and passed with good marks. I haven't discovered anything, not even an original interpretation of Canto XI of *Purgatorio*, which I have translated and written a commentary on."

"Why would you have to discover something? Your genius ought to be to fulfill yourself in the life you live, not in original analyses, discoveries, and interpretations. Your model ought to be Socrates or Goethe; but imagine a Goethe *without a written opus!*"

"I don't exactly understand," he said. ⚜ ⚜ ⚜

"Do you understand everything?" asked the Professor.

"I don't understand you very well, especially when you speak fast."

He understood very well. The Professor's French was impeccable; without doubt he had taken his doctorate in Paris. He seemed to speak more precisely and elegantly than the great specialist. Bernard was, probably, of foreign origin. But he guessed from his slow, hesitating sentences that — as Vaian had said about their last director, whenever he had had to make a grave decision quickly— he did not dare to express himself.

"When did you become convinced he's conscious?"

"Only the day before yesterday," said the Professor. "I had tried several times before to get a response, but without result."

"And you're *sure* he squeezed your finger? You *felt* him squeeze it in response to your question? Couldn't it have been a reflex gesture, involuntary and therefore without significance?"

"I repeated the experiment several times. Try it yourself, if you wish, and you'll be convinced."

He sensed, as at so many times in the past few days, a finger introduced gently, with exaggerated precaution, beneath his own fingers drawn up in a fist. Then he heard the Professor's voice: "If you understand what I am saying, squeeze my finger!" He must have squeezed it with sufficient force, because Dr. Bernard withdrew it quickly, surprised. But a few moments later, after whispering, "*Traduisez, s'il vous plait*," he introduced it again and said, pronouncing the words clearly and slowly: "*Celui qui vous parle est un médecin français. Accepteriez-vous qu'il vous pose quelques questions?*" Before the Professor had finished translating, he squeezed the finger as hard as before. This time the doctor did not withdraw it, but asked, "*Vous comprenez le français?*" He repeated the squeezing, but with less conviction. After hesitating a few moments, Dr. Bernard asked, "*Voulez-vous qu'on vous abandonne à votre sort?*" With great delight, he kept his whole hand inert, as if it were a plaster cast. "*Vous préférez qu'on s'occupe de vous?*" He squeezed hard. "*Voulez-vous qu'on donne du chloroforme?*" He immobilized his hand again, and kept it that way, without the slightest twitch, while listening to the final questions: "*Etes-vous Jésus-Christ? Voulez-vous jouer du piano? Ce matin, avez-vous bu du champagne?*"

༉ ༉ ༉ That night, everyone stood with champagne glasses in hand, surrounding them and shouting at them with a sad, mediocre lack of modesty that surprised them both: "Don't drink any more champagne till you get to Venice, or you'll be sick!"

"I was afraid that they drank more champagne than they should have," said Laura, after the train had left the station. ༄ ༄ ༄

Then he heard the Professor's voice: "Let's try one more time. Perhaps he didn't understand your questions properly. I'll question him in Romanian." And he continued, raising his voice. "We wish to find out your age. For every ten years squeeze my finger once."

He squeezed it, harder and harder, six times; then, without understanding why, he stopped.

"Sixty years?" marveled the Professor. "I'd have thought less."

"In this larval state," he heard the voice of Dr. Bernard saying, "it is hard to estimate. Ask him if he's tired, if we can continue."

They continued the dialogue for another half hour, learning by this means that he did not live in Bucharest, that he had only one relative, a distant one, whom he did not care to inform about the accident, that he would accept any test no matter how hazardous, to verify whether the optic nerve was damaged. Fortunately, they did not ask any more questions, because if they had he probably would not have listened to them. The blindness that threatened Papini had been the first sign. He had told himself, that week, that perhaps it was not a matter of the inevitable decrepitude of old age, that if he repeated the story of Papini (Papini, on whom no surgeon dared to operate), he did it because the tragedy of one of his favorite writers preoccupied him. But soon he realized he was trying to deceive himself. One year before that, Doctor Neculache had acknowledged that, for the time being, arteriosclerosis was incurable. The doctor had not told him that arteriosclerosis was threatening him, but he had added: "At a certain age, you can expect anything. I myself am losing my memory," he continued, smiling sadly. "From a certain time, I've been unable to memorize the verses of younger poets whom I discover and like."

"Nor can I," he had interrupted. "I once knew by heart the whole of *Paradiso*, and now . . . And as for the young writers, after I read them, I retain almost nothing."

And yet . . . Lately, as he lay there in bed with his eyes closed, he remembered many books he had read recently, and he mentally recited poems by Ungaretti, Ion Barbu, and Dan Botta — texts he hadn't realized he had ever memorized. As for *Paradiso*, for many days and nights he fell asleep reciting his favorite *terze rime.* He was seized suddenly by a strange fear, which he did not understand because it seemed to arise from the joy of the discovery he had made. Don't think anymore! he ordered himself. Think about something else! . . . And yet, for much of the time he did nothing else but recite poems and repeat books that he had read. I've been a blockhead! I was frightened for nothing! . . . Although, once when he had left the house he realized on reaching the street that he had forgotten where he wanted to go. . . . But perhaps it was just an accident. Perhaps I was tired . . . although I didn't have any reason to be tired.

"Actually, the great specialist didn't explain very much," he heard one of the interns saying.

"He did say that a few other cases are known. For instance, that Swiss pastor who was burned by lightning over almost his whole body and who nevertheless lived many years afterward. True, he was left mute — as our man is also, probably," he added, lowering his voice.

"Don't talk anymore; maybe he can hear you," whispered someone whose voice he could not identify.

"That's what I want — I want him to hear me. Let's see how he'll react. Perhaps he isn't mute after all."

Involuntarily, without realizing what he was doing, he slowly opened his mouth. At that moment he heard exceptionally loud noises in his ears, as if on both sides of him several freight cars loaded with scrap iron were tumbling down a rocky mountainside. But even though the echo of the explosions kept ringing in his ears, he continued to hold open his mouth. And suddenly he heard himself articulating, "No!" He repeated the word several times. Then after a short pause, he added, "Not mute!" He knew he had meant to say, "I'm not mute," but he had not succeeded in pronouncing the syllable "I'm." From the noises in the room and the sound of the door opening and closing quickly he understood that the two words had provoked a sensation. He held his mouth wide open, but he dared not move his tongue. When Doctor Gavrilă, his favorite, the one about whom he had been sure from the first that he had a medical vocation, approached the bed, he repeated the words again. Then he understood why he had so much difficulty pronouncing them: with each movement of the tongue he could feel his teeth rattling, as though they were ready to fall out.

"That was it," whispered Gavrilă. "The teeth. Even the molars," he added with a preoccupied air. "Call Dr. Filip on the telephone. Tell him to send someone immediately — ideally, he himself should come — and have him come prepared with everything necessary."

Then he heard him speaking at a distance.

"They're barely holding. If he were to swallow very hard, he'd be in danger of choking on a molar. Tell the Professor."

He felt pincers of some sort grasping a tooth in front and pulling it out without effort. He began to count: in a few minutes, with the same ease, Dr. Filip had extracted nine incisors and five molars.

"I don't exactly understand what's happened. The roots are healthy. It's as though they were being pushed out by wisdom teeth. But that's impossible. We'll have to take an X-ray."

The Professor stepped to the bed and put two fingers on the patient's right hand.

"Try to pronounce something, any word, any sound."

He tried moving his tongue without fear now, but he did not succeed in saying what he meant. Finally, resigned, he began to pronounce at random various short words: pin, cock, cow, man, pen, foam.

The third night after that, he had a dream he remembered completely. He had returned unexpectedly to Piatra Neamț and was on his way to lycée. But the closer to school he came, the more pedestrians there were. He recognized around him on the sidewalk many of his former pupils, looking as they did when he and they had parted, ten, twenty, or twenty-five years before. He took one of them by the arm. "Where are you all going in this crowd, Teodorescu?" he asked. The boy gave him a long look, smiling quizzically; he did not recognize him. "We're not going to school. Today is the centenary of Professor Dominic Matei."

*I don't like that dream very much, he repeated to himself several times. I don't understand why, but I do not like it.*

He waited for the nurse to leave. Then, with high emotion and great caution, he began to half-open his eyelids. He had found himself one night looking at a luminous, bluish spot, without realizing he had opened his eyes and without understanding what he was seeing. He felt his heart racing fast, frightened — and quickly he closed his eyes. But the next night he awoke again, staring with eyes opened wide at the same luminous spot. Not knowing what to do, he began counting mentally. When he reached 72, he suddenly realized that the light was coming from the venetian blind at the other end of the room. He could hardly control the happiness he felt looking, unhurriedly, one wall at a time, at his room, the one to which he had been transferred on the eve of Dr. Bernard's visit. After that, whenever he was left alone, especially at night, he would open his eyes, move his head slightly, then his shoulders, and begin to investigate the forms and colors, shadows and half-lights, around him.

"Why haven't you showed *us* that you could open your eyes?" It was the voice of one of the interns. In the next moment he saw him, and he was almost as he had imagined him by the inflections of his voice: tall, dark, lean, with the beginning of a bald spot. So, the intern had suspected something and had kept watch for a long time, to catch him.

"I don't know w'y," he replied, pronouncing his words only partially. "Maybe I wan'ed to convin' myself firs' that I hadn' los' my sigh'."

The intern looked at him, smiling vacantly.

"You, sir, are a curious man. When the Professor asked you your age, you answered sixty."

"I'm older."

"That's hard to believe. You heard, no doubt, what the nurses said."

With the respectful gesture of a repentant schoolboy, he inclined his head. He had heard them: "How old did he say he was — sixty? That man's hiding his age. You saw him this morning, a little while ago, when I was bathing him. He's a young man, in the prime of life; he's less than forty."

"I don't want you to think I spied on you so I could report you to the Director. But I must inform the Professor. And he will decide...."

Another time he would have been angry or afraid, but now he found himself reciting — at first mentally, then slowly moving his lips — one of his favorite poems, *La morte meditata*, by Ungaretti:

*Sei la donna che passa*
*Come una foglia*
*E lasci agli alberi un fuoco d'autunno. . . .* *

He remembered that when he had read that poem for
the first time, they had been separated for a long while
already: almost twenty-five years. And yet, reading it, he
had thought of her. He did not know if it was the same
love he had had at the beginning, if he loved her still as
he had confessed on the morning of October 12, 1904,
after they had left the courthouse and were headed for
Cişmigiu. When they parted, kissing her hand he had
added: "I wish you . . . Oh, you know what I mean. . . . But
I'd like you to know something else, that I'll love you till
I die." He was not sure he still loved her, but it was of her
he thought when he read, "*Sei la donna che passa . . .*"

"So, you're persuaded that you're out of danger
now."

Thus the Professor greeted him the next morning,
approaching him with a smile. He was more impressive
than he had imagined. Though not very tall, his manner
of holding his head high and his body erect, as though he
were on parade, gave him a somewhat intimidating mar-
tial air. If his hair had not been almost white, he would
have seemed severe. Even when he smiled he remained
grave, distant.

---

*You are the woman who passes / like a leaf / and leaves on the trees the fire
of autumn . . .

"Only now do you begin to become an 'interesting case,'" he added, seating himself on a chair facing the bed. "I believe you understand why. Up to now no one has found any plausible explanation, neither here nor abroad. The way the lightning struck you, you *had* to have been killed on the spot, or else to have died of asphyxiation in ten or fifteen minutes; at best you would have been left paralyzed, mute, or blind. The enigmas that confront us multiply with each passing day. I don't know to what reflex to attribute your inability to open your mouth for twenty-three days so that you had to be fed intravenously. Probably you succeeded in opening it when you had to eliminate your teeth, which your gums could no longer retain. We had planned to make a set of dentures to allow you to eat and above all to speak normally. But for the time being we can do nothing; the X-rays show that in a short time a whole new set of teeth will be ready to appear."

"Imposs'ble!" he exclaimed, dumbfounded, mutilating the word.

"So say all the doctors and dentists — that it is simply impossible. And yet the X-rays are quite clear. That is why, finally, I said that only now does your case become extremely interesting. No longer is it a case of a 'living dead man,' but of something else entirely. *What*, exactly, we still don't know."

I must be careful, I mustn't make a mistake and give myself away. Today, tomorrow they'll ask my name, address, occupation. Still, what have I to be afraid of? I haven't done anything. No one knows about the white

envelope or the blue envelope. . . . And yet, without
knowing why, he wanted at all costs to preserve his anonymity, the way it had been at first when they had shouted at him, "Do you hear me or not? If you understand
what I'm saying, squeeze my finger." Fortunately, now,
without any teeth, he spoke with difficulty. It would
be easy to pretend, to mangle those few words he managed to pronounce. But what if they asked him to write?
He looked at his right arm and right hand closely for the
first time. The skin was smooth, fresh, and was beginning
to acquire again its old coloring. He felt the arm slowly, cautiously, up to the elbow; then with two fingers he
caressed his biceps. How odd! Perhaps the almost absolute immobility for nearly four weeks, and those nutri-
tive fluids they injected directly into the veins . . . "He's a
young man, in the prime of life!" the nurse had said. And a
day before, he had heard a door being opened cautiously,
then steps approaching his bed, and the intern whispering, "He's asleep, don't wake him." Then a strange voice,
hoarse: "It can't be he. . . . Still, we'll have to see him without the beard. But the guy we were looking for is a student, not past twenty-two, and this man here looks older, close to forty."

Then he remembered again about the storm. "The curious thing about it," one of the interns had said, "was that
it was raining only in that one place where he was walking, between the North Station and bulevardul Elisabe-
ta. It was a sudden shower, like in the middle of summer,
which lasted long enough to flood the boulevard, but a

few hundred meters away — not a drop!" "That's true," someone had added. "I passed there on my way back from church, and the water on the boulevard still hadn't drained away." "Some say there was an attempt at a bombing, because supposedly a lot of dynamite was found, but the torrential rain caught them by surprise and they had to give it up." "That could be an invention of the Security, to justify their arresting students." Then they had all fallen silent.

I must be very careful, he repeated to himself. They might confuse me with one of the hidden Legionaries* the Siguranţă (Security) is looking for. And then I'll have to tell them who I am. They'll send me to Piatra to verify it. And then . . . But, as usual, he succeeded in uprooting the thought that annoyed him. He found himself reciting Canto XI from *Purgatorio*; then he tried to remember the passage from the *Aeneid: Agnosco veteris vestigia flammae* . . .

֍ ֍ ֍ "The trouble with you, *Cucoane*** Dominic, is that you never finish anything you start. You jump from one book to another, from one language to another, from one science to another. Perhaps that's why you two separated," he added with a sad smile.

---

*Members of an extreme rightist, nationalistic movement, also known as the Iron Guard, against which a massive crackdown had been ordered by the Romanian government in the spring of 1938, the time when the action of *Youth Without Youth* starts.

**Respectful form of address to an older man in Romanian *(archaic)*.

He had not been angry then. Nicodim was someone he liked, a good Moldavian, honest and quiet.

"No, Domnule* Nicodim, the Japanese language manual had nothing to do with our separating."

"What's this about a manual of Japanese?" Nicodim asked, surprised.

"I thought that was what you were referring to, to the rumor that circulated in the square."

"Which was—?"

"It was said that when I came home with a Japanese language manual, Laura, seeing me open my notebook immediately and begin to study, said . . . well, in short, she's supposed to have said that I started too many things and didn't carry any of them to a finish; and on account of this we separated."

"No, I never heard that. What I heard from one person and another is that Duduia** Laura became rather tired of your gallant adventures; that, in particular, this past summer in Bucharest you went around all the time with a French girl, saying that you knew her from your Sorbonne days."

"No," he interrupted wearily, shaking his head slowly. "That was something else entirely. It's true that Laura was suspicious, because she had found out about another, earlier affair, but she's an intelligent woman; she knows I don't *love* anyone but her; and that the others,

---

*Form of polite address to a man in Romanian.

**Respectful form of address to an unmarried young woman.

23

well . . . But I must tell you also that we've remained very good friends."

But he had not told him anything else. He had not told anyone, not even Dadu Rareş, his best friend, who died of tuberculosis twelve years later. Although Dadu, perhaps, had been the only one who had guessed the truth. Maybe Laura had even confided something to him, because they were very congenial. . . . ॐ ॐ ॐ

"I'm listening to you," said the Professor with a slight irritation in his voice. "I'm listening to you and I don't understand. For several days now, no progress. It even seems to me that last week you could pronounce certain words that today . . . You must cooperate with us. Don't be afraid of reporters. The orders are strict: no one will interview you. Obviously, your case was too important not to have become known in the city. News stories and feature articles have appeared in different papers, the majority of them absurd, ridiculous. But to return to the point, you *must* cooperate. We have to know more about you: where you're from, who you are, what your profession is, and so on."

He nodded his head obediently and repeated several times, "Yes, yes." This was no joke. He had to be on the lookout. Luckily, the next morning, while running his tongue over his gums, he felt the point of the first canine. With an exaggerated innocence, he showed it to the nurses, then to the interns, pretending it was impossible to say anything else. But the teeth appeared rapidly, one after another. By week's end, all of them had emerged. Every morning a dentist came to examine him and took notes for the article he was preparing. For several days he suffered with gingivitis, and even if he had wished, he could not have spoken very well. Those were the most serene days, because he felt, likewise, an energy and a confidence that he had not known since the time of the Great War, when at Piatra Neamț he had organized a "Movement of Cultural Renaissance" (so the local newspaper dubbed it), unequaled anywhere else in Moldavia. Even Nicolae Iorga had spoken of it with praise in a lecture he gave at the lycée. Professor Iorga had spent part of an afternoon at his house, and he had not hidden his surprise on discovering those many thousands of volumes of Orientalia, classical philology, ancient history, and archeology. "Why do you not write, colleague?" he had asked him several times. "I have been working, Domnule Professor. I have labored for some ten years to finish a work." Then Davidoglu had interrupted him with his inevitable joke: "But ask him, Domnule Professor, what kind of work! *De omni re scribili!*" It was an old joke of theirs, which they repeated every time they saw him coming to the office with a bundle of new books freshly arrived from Paris, Leipzig, or Oxford. "When do you plan to stop, Cucoane Dominic?" they would ask him. "How can I stop, when I haven't even reached the halfway point yet?" As a matter of fact he knew, in those days before the War, that by spending what little funds he had left on expensive books and study trips, he was obliged to remain a teacher there, in the lycée, and that consequently a good part of his time would be wasted with preparing lessons. For a long time Latin and Italian had ceased to interest him; he would have liked, if it had been possible, to give himself over to the history of civilization or to philosophy. "The way you want to do everything, ten lives wouldn't be enough." Once he had replied, almost with conviction: "I'm sure of one thing, at least: that for philosophy you do not need ten lives." "*Habe nun ach! Philosophie ... durchaus studiert!*"* the professor of German cited solemnly. "You know the rest," he added.

From the indiscretions of the assistants, he understood why the Professor was so on edge: Bernard was pressing him all the time for more ample and more precise information. "*En somme, qui est ce Monsieur?*" he asked in a letter. (But that was not certain, someone had observed. Dr. Gavrilă had said it, but he had not seen the letter.) Of course, Bernard had found out long before that the unknown person whom he had examined at the beginning of April had not lost his sight and that he had begun to speak. He was more curious now than ever. Not only the stages of the physical restoration but also as many details as possible about the patient's mental capacities interested him. The fact that the patient understood French led him to believe that he was a man of some education. He wanted to find out what he had retained and what he had lost. He suggested a series of tests: vocabulary, syntax, word associations.

---

*If only I had! Studied philosophy ... thoroughly!"

☸ ☸ ☸ "But when will you finish it, Domnule?"

"I still have to write the first part; the other parts—Antiquity, the Middle Ages, and the Modern Era—are almost completely written. But the first part—you understand, the origin of language, of society, of the family, of all the other institutions—this calls for years and years of research. And with our provincial libraries . . . I used to buy as many books as I could find, but now, with straitened means . . ."

As a matter of fact, the more time passed the more clearly he understood that he would never be able to finish his one and only book, his life's work. He awoke one morning with the taste of ashes in his mouth. He was approaching age sixty, and he had finished nothing of all that he had begun. Meanwhile, his "disciples," as some of his very young colleagues, overwhelmed with admiration, liked to call themselves, who had gathered at least one evening each week in the library to hear him speak about the enormous problems he had to resolve—his disciples had scattered with the passing of the years, moving to other cities. There was no one left even to entrust with the manuscripts and the materials he had collected.

When he heard that at the cafe they called him the Old Man or Papa Dominic, he realized that the prestige he had acquired during the War years, when Nicolae Iorga had praised him at the beginning of the lecture and had sent him now and then from Iaşi a student to request books from him—that prestige had begun to pale. Little by little he realized that in the faculty office or at the Cafe

Select he was no longer the center of attention, that he no longer "shone" as formerly. Recently, since he overheard Vaian saying, "The Old Man's really getting decrepit!" he had hardly dared speak about the new books he had read, about articles in *NRF, Criterion*, or *La Fiera Letteraria*. And then there had followed, one after the other, what he called in his secret language, "crises of consciousness."

"But what are you doing here, Domnu' Matei?"

"I'm taking a walk. A migraine hit me again, and I went out for a walk."

"But like this, in your pajamas, on Christmas Eve? Don't catch cold!"

The next day the whole city found out about it. Probably they were waiting for him at the cafe, to cross-examine him — but that day he didn't go, nor the next.

"At the first opportunity!" he exclaimed one afternoon in front of the Cafe Select, laughing. "At the first opportunity!"

"What will you do at the first opportunity?" Vaian queried him.

Indeed, what would he do? He frowned, trying to remember. At last he shrugged and set off for home. Not until he had put his hand on the door knob did he remember: At the first opportunity he would open the blue envelope. But not here, where everyone knows me. Far away, in another city. In Bucharest, perhaps. ༃ ༃ ༃

One morning he asked the nurse for a piece of paper, a pencil, and an envelope. He wrote a few lines, sealed the envelope, and addressed it to the Professor. Then he began to wait, sensing the rate of his heartbeat accelerating.

When before had he experienced a similar emotion? Perhaps on the morning when he had learned that Romania had declared a general mobilization. Or earlier, twelve years earlier, when, as he entered the parlor, he realized that Laura was waiting for him and that she wished to speak with him. It had seemed to him then that her eyes were moist.

༄ ༄ ༄ "I have to talk to you," she began, forcing a smile. "It's very important for both of us, and I can't hide it any longer. . . . It has to be brought out into the open. I felt this a long while ago, but for some time now it has obsessed me. I sense that you aren't *mine* any longer. Please, don't interrupt. It's not what you think . . . . I sense that you are not mine, that you aren't *here* with me, that you live in another world. I'm not thinking of your research, which, in spite of what you believe, *does* interest me. But I feel you're living in an alien world, one I cannot enter with you. Both for my sake and for yours, I believe it would be wiser for us to separate. We're still young, we both love life. . . . You'll see later. . . ." ༄ ༄ ༄

"Very well," said the Professor, after he had folded the paper carefully and inserted it into his appointment book. "I shall return later."

An hour later he returned. Locking the door in order not to be disturbed, he sat down on the chair facing the bed.

"I'm here to listen to you. It's not necessary that you make a very great effort. The words you can't pronounce you can write," he added, handing him a pad of paper.

"You will understand why I must resort to this stratagem," he began, obviously tense. "I wish to avoid publicity. The truth is this: my name is Dominic Matei. On January 8 I reached the age of seventy. I was instructor in Latin and Italian at Lycée Alexandru Ion Cuza in Piatra Neamț, where I now reside. I live on strada Episcopiei at No. 18. It is my house and it contains a library of nearly 8,000 volumes, which I have willed to the lycée."

"Extraordinary!" exclaimed the Professor, after taking a deep breath. He looked at the patient again, somewhat frightened it seemed.

"I believe it will not be hard for you to verify my story. But, I implore you, be very, very discreet! The whole city knows me. If you wish additional proof, I can draw you a plan of the house, I can tell you what books are on the desk and any other detail you ask me for. But, at least for the time being, it isn't necessary for anyone to know what's happened to me. As you yourself said, it's a rather sensational thing that I've escaped safe and sound. If it were to be learned that I've been hospitalized, I'd have no peace. I'm telling you all this because agents from Security who have been here already will never believe I'm past seventy. Therefore, they won't believe I am who I am, and I'll be interrogated — and anything can happen if you are interrogated! . . . I pray you, if you consider that my case deserves to be studied — I mean, that it deserves to be studied over a period of time here at the hospital — please find me a fictitious identity. Of course, it will be temporary, and if, later on, you become dissatisfied with my conduct, you may reveal the truth at any time."

"That's no problem," the Professor interrupted. "For the time being, the one thing that matters is for you to have a regular situation. This, I hope, will not be too hard to obtain. But what age can we give you? When we shave off your beard, you'll look like a man of thirty or thirty-one. Shall we say thirty-two?"

He asked the street and number of the house again, and noted them in his date book.

"The house, of course, is closed?" he began again after an interval.

"Yes and no. An old woman, Veta, my housekeeper for my whole life, lives in two little rooms attached to the kitchen. She keeps the keys for the other rooms."

"Probably there is an album of photographs somewhere, more precisely with pictures of you when you were young."

"All of them are in the upper drawer of the desk; there are three albums. The key to the drawer is under the cigar box on top of the desk. . . . But if the person you send says anything to Veta, the whole city will find out."

"There's no danger if he proceeds with caution."

He returned the date book to his pocket pensively and was silent a few moments, keeping his eyes on Dominic all the while.

"I admit, your case excites me," he said, getting up. "I don't understand it, and neither does anyone else at the hospital. Probably you do exercises when you're alone at night."

He shrugged his shoulders, embarrassed.

"I felt my legs were 'asleep,' so I got out of bed and here, on the rug . . ."

"Didn't anything surprise you?"

"Yes, indeed. I felt of myself all over. I sensed my muscles were as they were years ago, strong, robust. I didn't expect that. After so many weeks of almost absolute immobility, it would have to be, how to say it? a sort of . . ."

"Yes, it would have to be that," the Professor interrupted. He started toward the door, but stopped, turned, and sought his eyes. "You didn't give me any address for here, in Bucharest."

He felt himself blushing, but with an effort he managed to smile. "I have no address, because I'd scarcely arrived. I came by train from Piatra Neamţ. It was almost midnight when I arrived, the night of Easter."

The Professor stared at him in disbelief.

"But you must have been going somewhere. And on the sidewalk, next to you, there was no valise found."

"I didn't have a valise. I brought nothing with me except a blue envelope. I had come with the intention of committing suicide. It seemed to me I was a condemned man: arteriosclerosis. I was losing my memory."

"You came here to commit suicide?" the Professor echoed.

"Yes. I saw no other solution. The only solution was the blue envelope. I had been keeping there, for a long time, a few milligrams of strychnine."

# 2

He knew he was dreaming, and he kept wiping his hand across his freshly shaved cheek, but he did not succeed in fully waking up. Only after the car had reached the end of the boulevard did he recognize the neighborhood; he recognized it mainly by the fragrance of the lindens in flower. We're headed toward Şosea, he realized. He had not passed through here for several years and, moved, he gazed at the old houses, which reminded him of his student years. Then they entered an avenue lined with tall trees; the following moment a gate opened and the car, moving slowly over the gravel drive, came to a halt in front of stairs of bluish stone. "Why don't you get out?" he heard an unfamiliar voice asking. Looking around in surprise, he saw no one. It appeared that up above, at the head of the stairs, a door had opened. So, he was expected. I ought to get out, he said to himself.

Waking up, the bright light from outside blinded him, and he looked in surprise at the clock. It was not yet 6:00. Probably they forgot to draw the blinds. Presently he heard the door open.

"I've brought you your clothes," said the nurse, smiling as she approached the bed, her arms laden.

She was Anetta, still rather young, the most daring of the nurses. (A few days earlier she had said, "When you're released, maybe you'll take me to the cinema some evening!") She helped him dress, although he would not have needed any help. He guessed from her look of disappointment that the jacket didn't fit very well ("Too tight in the shoulders," she said) and the tie, blue with little gray triangles, did not go well with the striped shirt. Soon the intern in residence entered. He began to examine him carefully, frowning.

"It looks from a distance as though those are not your clothes. You could become suspect. We'll have to find you something else. Dr. Gavrilă said that he has some outfits of the best quality, left by an uncle of his."

"He inherited them after the uncle died," Anetta specified. "And it isn't good to wear clothes from other families' dead. From your own dead, it's different. You wear them in memory, as a souvenir."

"It doesn't matter," he said, smiling. "Anyway, there isn't time today. Perhaps on another occasion, when I pass this way again."

"Yes," the intern agreed, "but with that jacket you'll attract attention and risk being followed."

"If he hunches down in the back seat of the car, maybe he won't be noticed."

Two hours later he went downstairs and out into the courtyard, accompanied by Dr. Chirilă, the one he liked the least, because, after Chirilă had caught him opening his eyes that night, he had had the impression that the doctor was spying on him all the time. Setting eyes on the car, he stopped abruptly.

"I've seen that car before!" he whispered. "I saw it last night, in my dream. Some would say it's a bad sign, that we might have an accident."

"I am not superstitious," Dr. Chirilă proclaimed, speaking slowly and sententiously as he opened the car door. "In any event, they're waiting for us."

When the auto started for the boulevard, he felt a strange peace, broken now and then by almost violent upsurges of happiness.

"Open the window," he added. "Now we're approaching Şosea." And later: "Look at that beautiful building with the tall trees, and that neat drive with gravel, and the stairs of bluish stone."

The intern kept looking at him curiously, frowning silently. The car stopped in front of the steps.

"Why don't you get out?" he heard a voice saying.

"We're waiting for the orderly to come, to take charge," the driver replied.

Soon hurried footsteps were heard on the gravel, and from behind the car there appeared a bespectacled man, with a face pinched by age and hair close-cropped, military style. Chirilă opened the door.

"He is the person about whom you were informed. You are not to treat him like just another patient. From now on, you're responsible for him."

"I understand," he said. "Don't worry. I'll keep on the lookout."

"What he does inside or in the garden doesn't concern you. Your job is to guard the gate."

He liked the room: it was spacious, with windows opening on the park and, as the Professor had assured him, it had a wooden table and, on the walls, shelves for books. He stepped to the open window and breathed deeply. It seemed the fragrance of wild roses was reaching him from somewhere. Yet, he could not, somehow, feel happy. He smiled, caressing his left cheek with his hand, but it seemed to him that all that had happened for some time past did not concern him *really*, that it had to do with something else, with *someone* else.

"Try to describe, as precisely and with as many details as possible, what you mean when you say, 'Someone else,'" the Professor interrupted him once. "In what sense do you feel *alien* to yourself? Are you not yet 'installed' in your new situation? This is very important. Note down all that passes through your mind. If you aren't in the mood to write or if you have too much to say, use the recorder, indicating always the day, hour, and place, and specifying whether you are dictating while lying in bed or walking about your room."

During the last several days at the hospital he had filled almost a whole notebook. He wrote all kinds of things: books that he remembered (and he enjoyed indicating the edition, year of publication, and year when he had read it for the first time, in order to verify his miraculous recovery of memory), poems in all the languages he had learned, algebraic exercises, a few dreams that seemed significant. But some recent discoveries he did not confess. He sensed an incomprehensible resistance, about which he had spoken once with the Professor. "It's very important for us to learn the significance of this resistance," the Professor had said. "Try at least to make some allusion, so we will know if what you don't *want* to say (*cannot* say! he interjected mentally) refers to certain events from the past, or if it is a matter of something else having to do with your new condition — about which, I repeat, we still know very little."

He turned away from the window and, after pacing the room several times — walking as he used to do, in his youth, with his hands clasped behind his back — he stretched out on the bed. He lay there with his eyes open, staring at the ceiling.

"I've brought you your family album," the Professor said to him one morning. "The one with your pictures from lycée, the university, Italy. . . . Aren't you curious to see it?"

"To tell you the truth, no."

"But why?"

"I don't know why myself. I'm beginning to feel detached from my past. It's as though I weren't the same person."

"That's strange," said the Professor. "We ought to discover the reasons."

At last, resigned, he decided to leaf through it. The

Professor was sitting beside the bed, in a chair, watching him closely, incapable of concealing his curiosity.

"What are you thinking about?" he asked him abruptly after a few minutes. "What sort of memories? What sort of associations?"

He hesitated, rubbing his cheek with his left hand. ("I know that gesture has become a habit of mine, a tic," he had admitted several times.)

"I remember perfectly the year and location where they were taken, every one of them. I can even say I remember the *day;* it's as though I can hear the voices of those around me and the words they spoke, and I seem to sense in my nostrils the smell peculiar to that place and that day.... See here, for instance, where I'm with Laura, at Tivoli. When I set eyes on that snapshot, I felt the heat of that morning and the fragrance of the oleander flowers. But I sensed also a strong odor of hot crude oil, and I recalled that some twenty meters from the spot where we were photographed there were two pails of crude oil."

"It's a kind of hypermnesia with lateral effects," said the Professor.

"It's awful," he continued. "It's too much, and it's so useless!"

"It seems useless because we don't know yet what to do with it, with that fantastic recovery of memory.... In any event," he added, smiling, "I have good news for you. In a few days you will receive from your library at Piatra Neamț the books you noted on your first list, that is, all the grammars and dictionaries you said you'd need. Bernard is enthusiastic. He told me we couldn't find a more suitable test. He was interested especially in the fact that you began to study Chinese in your youth, then you neglected it for ten or twelve years, then you took it up again before and during the war years, and finally, quite suddenly, you gave it up completely. We have to deal, therefore, with several strata of the memory. If you will take pains to analyze yourself and make careful notes, we shall see which of the strata will be revived first."

For some time they looked at each other, as if each were waiting for the other to begin.

"And what do people at Piatra Neamţ believe about my disappearance?" he asked suddenly. "I'm not too curious, but I'd be interested to know about what my chances are now."

"What kind of chances?"

He smiled, embarrassed. As soon as he had uttered the expression it had seemed vulgar and inappropriate.

"My chances for continuing the life I recently began, without the risk of reintegrating it into my previous biography."

"For the time being, I can't tell you anything precise. Your friends in Piatra believe you are in a hospital in Moldavia, suffering from amnesia. Someone remembered that he saw you at the station on the Saturday before Easter, but he doesn't know what train you took; the man was in a hurry to get home."

"I have an idea who it was that saw me at the station," he whispered.

"In order to be able to collect the books you listed, the police staged a search. They pretended that, having learned of your disappearance, one of the wanted Legionaries might have hidden in your library."

He remained pensive for a while, as though reluctant to continue.

"But of course the more time passes, the more difficult it will get. Soon it will be learned at Piatra Neamț what all Bucharest knows: that someone, an older man of unknown origin, was struck by lightning and after ten weeks appeared perfectly healthy and young again. Let us hope the rest will not be found out."

Two weeks later, upon coming downstairs to the garden, he came face to face with a young woman of strange beauty — a beauty that, for reasons hard to grasp, she tried to attenuate by means of a deliberate vulgarity, applying makeup in an exaggerated and clumsy manner. The way she smiled at him then, provocatively and yet chastely, the girl reminded him of one of his most recent dreams. He inclined his head slightly and spoke.

"Haven't we met somewhere before?"

The young woman began to laugh. (Too bad, he said to himself, she laughs in the same vulgar way she paints her face.)

"You're as discreet as you can be!" she said. (And it seemed she spoke as if on stage.) "Of course we've met before; several times, in fact."

"Where? When?"

The young woman wrinkled her brow in a slight frown and sought his eyes again.

"Most recently, last night, in Room Number 6. Your room is next door, Number 4," she added, walking away.

The Professor came that same evening, to return the notebook and to read the latest notations. He listened, perplexed, confused, without smiling, avoiding his gaze.

"I believe you know what it's all about, and that you understand — how to say it? — the scientific intent of the experiment. No analysis is complete without the index of the sexual capacity. You remember the question Bernard asked you the last time. . . ."

He wanted to laugh, but succeeded only in nodding his head and smiling.

"Do I remember! I fell through the floor with shame! Naked, spread out on the table, in front of all those foreign doctors and scholars!"

"I warned you in advance that there would be a sort of international consultation. They all came on account of you. They couldn't believe the reports I published in *La Presse médicale*."

"I wasn't expecting such a question. Especially since I was still in the hospital and therefore didn't have any way to confirm or rule out the sexual possibilities."

The Professor smiled, giving a shrug.

"We found out something, of course, from the nurse."

"From the nurse?"

"We thought the initiative was yours. In any other circumstances, the patient and the nurse involved would have been penalized. But in your case, we not only shut our eyes, we valued the information. In the last analysis, the context doesn't matter. All that matters is the information. . . . But in the case of the young lady in Room 6," he resumed after a pause, "we have to do with something else. It's better I tell you now, lest complications arise later. That woman has been imposed on us by Security."

"By Security?" he repeated with some fear. "But why?"

"I don't claim to understand very much of it, but I *know* that Security is very interested in your case. Probably they aren't convinced that I've been telling the whole truth and actually, of course, they're right. At any rate, Security does not believe in your metamorphosis. They're convinced that the story circulating in the city about the lightning on Easter night, your unconsciousness, and your recovery of your health and youth is an invention of the Legionaries. They believe that in fact this legend was fabricated to camouflage the identity of an important Legionary leader and pave the way for his flight across the border."

He listened, surprised and yet serene.

"Then, my situation is graver than I had imagined," he said. "But since, for the time being, there is no other solution . . ."

"A solution will be found, in time," the Professor interrupted. "I must add, so that you may be better informed, that you are, and have been from the beginning, under the supervision of Security. That is why an outfit was procured for you in which you would not dare go out on the street because you would be arrested immediately. Neither would you dare to circulate in the city in that 'cassock,' the uniform of the clinic, which is, in fact, rather elegant. And, as you have understood from the first, if you want to walk, you can't go outside the gate. . . . This is what we know. But who can tell how many other members of the clinic staff are informers for Security?"

He began laughing and rubbed his left hand over his cheek several times.

"Actually, perhaps it's better this way. I feel safe from surprise."

The Professor sat looking at him for a long time, as though hesitating to say more. Then suddenly he decided to continue.

"Let us return, now, to a more important problem. Are you *sure* that, in your memory, all your sexual experiences have passed as erotic dreams?"

He was pensive for some moments.

"I'm not so sure any more. Up to this evening, I was convinced they were only dreams."

"I ask, because in your notebook which I read, you recorded all kinds of dreams, but without any *manifestly* erotic elements."

"Perhaps I should have noted the others too, but I didn't think they were significant. . . . In any event," he continued after a short pause, "if I've confused real experiences with erotic dreams, things are more complicated than I had imagined."

With a childish, almost ridiculous gesture he put his

hand to his temple as if he wanted to show he was concentrating.

"I'm listening," said the Professor at length. "In what sense could they be more complicated than they seem to be?"

He raised his head suddenly and smiled a puzzled smile.

"I don't know whether or not you understood certain allusions in the notebook, but for some time I've had the impression — how to say it? — I've had the impression that I was learning during the time I'm asleep; more precisely, I dream that I'm studying. For instance, I open a grammar in my dream, I read over and memorize several pages, or I leaf through a book. . . ."

"Very interesting!" said the Professor. "But I don't believe you've recorded all these things with precision and clarity in your notebook."

"I don't exactly know how to describe them. They were a series of dreams, in a sense didactic, and they seemed to be continuations of readings done during the day. I even thought I was dreaming grammatical rules, vocabulary, and etymologies, because I used to have a passion for such things. . . . But now I wonder if in a more or less somnambulic way I get up during the night and continue my work."

The Professor continued to stare at him closely, frowning slightly — a sign, as he had observed long ago, that he was tempted by several questions at the same time.

"In any event," he said, "you don't seem tired, you

don't have the expression of an intellectual who spends a good part of the night reading. . . . But if it were true, why hasn't anyone noticed a light, a lamp burning late in your room?"

He rose from the armchair and extended his hand.

"What seems paradoxical to me is the fact that this hesitation, more precisely this confusion between oneiric experiences and the waking state, has developed in parallel with your hypermnesia. . . . What you said to me then about the smell of oleanders and crude oil that you sensed while looking at a picture taken almost forty years ago . . ."

"But now I'm not sure about that any more!" he exclaimed. "I'm not sure about anything now!"

After the Professor had gone, he found himself thinking: *It was a good thing that you said, I'm not sure about anything anymore. In that way, you're always covered. You can answer anytime, I dreamed it! Or when it's convenient you can say the opposite. But watch out! Don't ever tell the* WHOLE *truth!*

He turned his head and looked around in surprise. A few moments later he whispered as if he were addressing someone present, yet invisible: "But even if I wanted to tell, *I couldn't!* I don't understand why," he added, lowering his voice even more, "but certain things are impossible for me to say."

That night he wrestled a long while with insomnia. (It was his first insomnia since he had left Piatra Neamţ, and that fact annoyed him. He had suffered from insomnia almost all his life, and recently he believed he was cured of it.) As usual, he thought about the mystery of his recovered memory. In fact, he realized, it was not just a matter of a recovery, because his memory now was more extensive and more precise than it had ever been. "The memory of a Mandarin," as Chavannes had said every Sinologue needed. He had begun to believe he had even more than that: a hypermnesia. Even before the grammars and dictionary had been brought him from Piatra, he found himself one day reciting Chinese texts, at the same time visualizing the characters and translating as fast as he recited. Several days later he verified the ideograms, pronunciation, and translation by using Giles's anthology and dictionary. He had not made a single mistake! He wrote several lines in a notebook, with a slight feeling of regret: Bernard would be disappointed. It was impossible to specify which stratum of the memory had appeared first. He found himself suddenly in possession of the Chinese language, as he had never known it before. Now he could open any text, and reading it understand it as easily as he could a text in Latin or Old Italian.

It was a very warm night and he had left open the window facing the park. Thinking he heard footsteps, he got out of bed and without turning on the light crept to the window. Outside he saw the orderly and he realized the man had seen him too.

"Don't you ever sleep?" he asked, speaking as softly as possible in order not to wake the others.

The orderly shrugged, then moved off toward the park, becoming lost in the darkness. If I ask him about it tomorrow, he said to himself, probably, he'll tell me I was dreaming. And yet I'm *certain* this time that I'm not dreaming. He went back to bed and said to himself, as he used to do when he was suffering from insomnia: In three minutes I'll be asleep! *You must go to sleep*, he heard himself thinking, *because in sleep you learn best of all. Didactic dreams, as the Professor said this evening. You must have another series of didactic dreams, not related to Chinese, but to something else, something more important!*

He liked to listen to himself think, but this time he sensed a mysterious uneasiness, and he whispered to himself threateningly: If you don't go to sleep by the count of twenty, I'll go down and take a walk in the park! But he got no further than the number seven.

Several days later the Professor asked him, without lifting his eyes from the second book of notes: "Do you remember that one night you climbed out the window and walked to the back of the garden where the beds of roses are located?"

He sensed himself blushing, and he felt intimidated. "No. I *do* remember that I couldn't go to sleep, and at a certain moment I said to myself, 'If you don't go to sleep by the count of twenty, I'll go down and take a walk in the park!' After that I remember nothing. Probably I fell asleep immediately."

The Professor smiled at him enigmatically. "In any event, you didn't fall asleep immediately.... Because you spent a period of time in the vicinity of the roses."

"Then I'm a sleepwalker!" he exclaimed. "For the first time in my life I've had an attack of somnambulism!"

The Professor got up suddenly, strode to the window, and stood staring straight ahead for some time. Then he returned to the armchair and reseated himself.

"That's what I thought, too. But things are not so simple. When the orderly gave the alarm, two staff members — probably Security agents — ran to search the street, not knowing the orderly had discovered you already. They saw a car with its headlights turned off waiting in the street, right in front of the rose bed where you were found. Of course, the auto disappeared before they could get the license number."

He put his hand to his forehead and removed it again, nervously. "If I didn't know you, . . ." he began.

"I know, it seems incredible," interrupted the Professor. "Nevertheless, there are three witnesses, simple men but trustworthy and experienced."

"And what did they do with me? Did they take me back to my room?"

"No, there was no one but the orderly in the garden. He says that as soon as you caught sight of him, you went back to the house. You climbed into your room through the window, the way you had left. . . . Sleepwalking or not, it doesn't matter. The serious thing is that Security no longer doubts an escape is being planned for you. The fact that you were caught in the very place where, on the street, a car was waiting, proves, in their opinion, that you knew what was going on and were in agreement with it. I had to intercede for you in high places to prevent your being arrested."

"Thank you," he said with some embarrassment, wiping his forehead.

"Meanwhile, they've doubled their guard. The street is patrolled continually all night; a sergeant in street clothes will look after things during working hours right outside your window — as he is doing now," he added, lowering his voice, "while at night the orderly will sleep on a folding cot in the corridor outside your door."

He stood up again and began pacing the floor, absently passing the notebook from one hand to the other. Suddenly he halted in front of him and looked him deeply in the eyes.

"But how do you explain this series of coincidences: for the first time you have insomnia, followed, as you admit, by the first attack of somnambulism you ever had in your life; at the time of the attack you head straight for the rose bed, *exactly* in the place where, across the wall, a car is waiting with its lights out. A car that," he added after a few moments, "disappeared immediately after the alarm was given. How do you explain all that?"

He shrugged his shoulders, discouraged. "I don't understand it at all. Until last week it was hard for me to admit that I'd confused some dreams with the waking state; I had to be convinced by certain evidence. But this time... an attack of somnambulism, the car waiting for me..."

The Professor opened his almost-full briefcase and slipped the notebook carefully between the magazines and pamphlets.

"To repeat an expression you used a little while ago,

if I didn't know you from your family picture albums, if I hadn't seen photographs of you from thirty to sixty-some years, I'd be ready to accept the hypothesis of Security: that you are who Security thinks you are. . . ."

*Why are you so agitated?* he heard himself thinking once the light was out. *Everything is unfolding normally. It had to happen like this, for you to be confused with others, to have people think you can't distinguish dream from reality, and other confusions of the same sort. You couldn't have found a better camouflage. Ultimately, you will be convinced that there is no danger, that you can behave without worry.*

He broke off abruptly; then, after a short pause, he whispered, "Who is taking care of me?" He waited several moments. Then he found himself asking in an unfamiliar voice, *Do you think that all you've gone through is due to chance? It's not a question of what I believe or what I don't believe,* he interrupted himself crossly. *Who is it that is watching over me?* Again he waited for some time, with fear. Then he heard: *You'll find out later. That doesn't matter now. Besides, you've guessed some of it, but you don't dare admit it. Otherwise, why don't you ever say anything to the Professor about* CERTAIN THOUGHTS, *and why don't you mention them in your notebook? If you didn't know* SOMEONE ELSE *existed, why don't you refer to all that you've discovered in the past two weeks? But, to return to my question* . . . , he tried to interrupt his thought. He waited a while, and when it seemed that he was beginning to distinguish the response, he fell asleep.

*It is better we talk in dreams,* he heard. *While you are sleeping, you understand more quickly and more profoundly. You told the Professor that in sleep you continue the studies of the daytime. As a matter of fact, you were convinced long ago that this is not always true. You haven't learned anything, either while sleeping or while waking. Little by little you discovered you had mastered Chinese, just as you discovered later you had mastered other languages that interested you. You no longer dare to believe that you are remembering NOW what you learned in youth and forgot. Think about the Albanian grammar!*

The memory of this struck him so forcefully that he awakened from sleep and turned on the light. He could not believe it then, and he could scarcely believe it now, a week after the discovery. He knew he had never studied the Albanian language. True, he had purchased G. Meyer's *Grammar* some twenty years ago, but he had never read further than the preface. Nor had he consulted it since that time. And yet when he unwrapped one of the packages brought from Piatra and set eyes on it, he opened it at random toward the end of the book and began to read. With a thrill and a fright, he realized he understood everything he was reading. He looked up the translation of the paragraph and he was convinced: not a mistake! He got out of bed and stepped to the bookshelves. At all costs he must verify it again, now. Just then he heard an unfamiliar voice coming from outside the open window.

"But aren't you sleeping?"

He returned to bed, shut his eyes with fury, and repeated in a whisper, "I must not think! I mustn't think of anything!"

*I said that to you on the first night at the hospital*, he heard.

He thought he was beginning to understand what had happened. The enormous concentration of electricity that, by exploding directly above him, had shot through him, had regenerated his entire organism and amplified fabulously all his mental faculties. But this electrical discharge had made possible likewise the appearance of a new personality, a sort of "double," a "person" whom he heard speaking to him especially during his sleep, with whom he sometimes had friendly discourse and sometimes disagreed. It was probable that this new personality had been built up gradually, during the time of his convalescence, from the deepest strata of his unconscious. Every time he repeated this explanation, he heard himself thinking, *Quite correct! The formula of the "double" is correct and useful. But don't be in a hurry to inform the Professor!*

He wondered, amused and vexed at the same time, why he kept repeating to himself such invitations to precaution when he had decided long ago not to touch this problem (in fact, it had not even been necessary for him to make a decision: he knew that he *could not* do otherwise). In conversations the Professor returned continually to hypermnesia and his progressive detachment from the past.

"We could bring you the manuscripts and portfolios with notes," he had proposed recently. "With the possibilities you have at your disposal now, you could finish the work in a few months."

He raised his arms high in a gesture of protest. "No, no!" he exclaimed, almost in panic. "It doesn't interest me any more!"

The Professor looked at him, surprised and somewhat disappointed. "But it's your life's work!"

"I would have to rewrite it from the first to the last page, and I don't believe it's worth it. It will have to remain what it was: an *opus imperfectum*. But there's something I'd like to ask you," he continued as if he wanted to change the subject as quickly as possible, "although I'm afraid I may seem indiscreet. What's been happening to me in the past week? What have the orderly and all the others reported?"

The Professor stood up and walked to the window without answering. He returned to the chair after a few moments, pensive.

"They know how to make themselves invisible when they need to, but they are all on duty," he said. "They haven't reported anything sensational: just that you turned on the light several times at night, then switched it off again quickly a few minutes later. . . . At least, so I have been informed. But I suspect they haven't told me everything," he added, lowering his voice. "I suspect they've found out something rather important, or they are on the road to discovering something. . . ."

"With regard to me?" he asked, successfully controlling his excitement.

The Professor hesitated a few moments, then rose suddenly and went to the window again. "I don't know," he answered at length. "It could be that it's not *only* with regard to you."

On the third of August he came to see him unexpectedly.

"I don't know if we ought to be happy or not. You've become famous in the United States. An illustrated magazine has even published an 'interview,' obviously apocryphal: 'How I Was Struck by Lightning.' The article created a sensation and has been reprinted and translated everywhere. From the Press Office I have been informed that three correspondents from large American dailies arrived last evening and insist on speaking with you. I told them that for the time being the doctors are against any visits. But how long will we be able to hide? It is likely that at this very hour the reporters have already begun their questioning. The interns and nurses will tell them all they know, and so will many others higher up. And they'll find informers here also," he added, lowering his voice. "With regard to the photographers, I have no illusions: you've been photographed certainly many times, walking in the park, standing at the window, perhaps even lying in bed. . . . But I see that this news doesn't impress you very much," he added after regarding him carefully. "You say nothing."

"I'm waiting for the sequel."

The Professor stepped closer, still looking him deeply in the eyes. "How do you know there is a 'sequel?'" he asked.

"I guessed it from your nervousness. I've never seen you so nervous."

The Professor shrugged and smiled bitterly. "You haven't seen me so, maybe, but I'm a rather nervous individual. . . . But to return to your case. A lot of complications have arisen, especially during the two weeks I was away."

"On account of me?" he asked.

"Not on your account, nor mine. You've stayed in your room almost the whole time (I know, because I telephoned nearly every day). As for me, in the two weeks I spent at Predeal, I did not discuss your case except with a few colleagues, of whose discretion I have no doubt. But something else has happened," he went on, rising from the chair. "First, the young lady from Room 6, the agent Security imposed on us, disappeared some ten days ago. Security suspected long ago that she was a double agent, but they did *not* suspect she was in the service of the Gestapo!"

"Very strange," he whispered. "But how was it learned so fast?"

"Because the network with which she was connected was discovered and three agents were arrested, the men who were waiting for you on several different nights in the car with its lights turned off. Security guessed rightly: you were to be abducted and passed across the border into Germany. They were wrong, however, about identities: it was not a matter of a Legionary leader, but *you*."

"But why?" he asked, smiling.

The Professor stepped to the window but quickly returned, looking at him closely, as though he expected him to say something more.

"Because you are the way you are, after all that has happened to you. I never entertained any illusions," he continued, beginning to pace slowly back and forth between the door and the chair. "I knew that one day it would be found out. That is why I also informed *La Presse médicale* in a few lines. I wanted what was learned to be learned directly from the source. Obviously, I didn't tell everything; I was content to report the stages of physical and intellectual re-establishment just by an allusion, and that rather obscure, to regeneration and rejuvenation. Nothing about the hypermnesia. But everything was found out: about your phenomenal memory and the fact that you've recovered all the languages you studied in your youth. Therefore, you have become the most valuable human specimen existing today on the face of the earth. All the medical schools in the world would like, at least temporarily, to have you at their disposal."

"A sort of guinea pig?" he asked, smiling.

"In certain cases, yes: a guinea pig. Having access to the information transmitted by the woman from Room 6, it is easy to understand why the Gestapo wants, at all costs, to abduct you."

He stood pensive for some moments, then suddenly his face brightened in a big smile.

"Your companion of a night, or several . . ."

"I'm afraid it was several," he admitted, blushing.

"Your companion was more intelligent than Security considered her. She was not content to test your sexual potential and, taking advantage of your parasomnambulic condition, she quizzed you, trying to decipher your identity. She proceeded scientifically: she recorded on a minuscule recording device all your conversations including, in fact, your long monologues, and she transmitted them to Security. But she noticed something else, too: for example, that you recited poems in a great many languages, and when she asked you questions in German and then in Russian, you replied without difficulty in the languages of the questions. Then, after you received the books, she made a list of all the grammars and dictionaries you had consulted. Wisely, she preserved all this information for her bosses in Germany. It is probable that after listening to the recordings someone high up in the Gestapo decided to kidnap you."

"I understand," he said, rubbing his forehead.

The Professor stopped in front of the open window, gazing out on the park.

"Of course," he added at length, "the guard has been increased tenfold. Probably you weren't aware of it, but for several days many of the neighboring rooms have been occupied by agents. At night, you can imagine how the street is patrolled. And yet, in spite of all this, soon you will have to be evacuated from here."

"Too bad!" he said. "I'm used to it — and I like it here."

"I have been advised to begin your camouflaging already. For the time being, you are to let your moustache grow as thick and bushy as possible. I've been told that they will try to modify your face. I imagine they'll also dye your hair and change your hair style, so that you will no longer resemble the photographs that have certainly been taken in recent weeks. They've assured me that they can add ten to fifteen years. When you leave the clinic, you'll look like a man in his forties."

He stopped speaking and sat down in the chair wearily.

"Fortunately," he added later, "those attacks of parasomnambulism, or whatever they were, have not recurred. At least, so I've been told."

The day promised to be torrid. He took off his robe and put on the thinnest pajamas he could find in the closet. Then he stretched out on the bed. *Of course*, he heard himself thinking, *you know very well it wasn't somnambulism. You've behaved as you had to, in order to create the necessary confusion. But from now on we won't need such devices.*

"The double," he whispered, smiling. "He always answers the questions I'm ready to ask him. Like a true guardian angel." *And that's a correct and useful formula.* Are there others? *Many. Some of them are anachronistic or out of use, others are rather current, especially in places where Christian theology and practice have known how to preserve the immemorial mythological traditions.* For example? he asked, amused. *For example, along with angels and guardian angels, there are Powers, Archangels, Seraphim, and Cherubim. Inter-*

*mediary beings par excellence.* Intermediary between consciousness and unconsciousness? *Of course. But also between Nature and man, between man and the divine, reason and Eros, feminine and masculine, darkness and light, matter and spirit.*

He came to, laughing, and sat bolt upright. For several moments he looked around, then whispered, pronouncing the words slowly: "So, I've come back again to my old passion, philosophy. Will I ever succeed in demonstrating logically the reality of the exterior world? Idealistic metaphysics still seems to me today to be the only perfectly coherent construct." *We've gotten off our subject,* he heard the voice say. *The problem was not the reality of the exterior world, but the objective reality of the "double" or the guardian angel — pick any term that suits you. Isn't that true?* Very true. I can't believe in the *objective* reality of the "person" with whom I'm conversing; I consider him my "double." *In a sense, that's what he is. But that doesn't mean he does not exist in an objective way, independently of the consciousness whose projection he appears to be.* I'd like to be convinced, but . . . *I know, in metaphysical controversies empirical proofs have no value. But wouldn't you enjoy receiving, right now, in a moment or two, a few fresh roses picked from the garden?* Roses! he exclaimed with feeling and some trepidation. I've always liked roses. *Where would you like me to put them? Not in the glass, at any rate.* . . . No, he replied. Not in the glass. But a rose in my right hand, as I'm holding it now, open, and another on my knee. And a third, let's say. . . .

At that moment he suddenly found himself holding

between his fingers a beautiful rose the color of fresh blood, and on his knee, in an unstable balance, another was rocking. *And the third?* he heard himself thinking. *Where do you want me to put the third rose?*

"Things are more serious than we anticipated," he heard the voice of the Professor saying. It seemed he was hearing it through a thick pillow, or else that it was coming from very far away. And yet he was right there in front of him, in the easy chair, with the briefcase on his lap.

"More serious than we anticipated?" he echoed absently.

The Professor stood up, went to him, and put a hand on his forehead. "Don't you feel well?" he asked. "Did you have a bad night, perhaps?"

"No, no. But just now, when you entered the room, it seemed . . . Actually . . ."

"I must speak to you of something urgent and very important," the Professor continued. "Have you come to your senses? Do you think you can listen?"

He wiped his hand slowly across his forehead and, with an effort, managed to smile. "I'm even very curious to listen to you."

The Professor sat down in the chair again. "I said that the situation is more serious than we suspected, because now we know the Gestapo will try anything — *anything*," he repeated, emphasizing the word, "in order to get their hands on you. You will understand why immediately. Among the intimates of Goebbels there is an enigmatic and ambiguous personage, a certain Dr. Rudolf, who for the past several years has been elaborating a theory that on first view is fantastic, but incorporates certain scientific elements also. He believes that electrocution by a current of at least a million volts could produce a radical mutation of the human species. Not only would the person submitted to such an electrical discharge not be killed, but he would be completely regenerated. . . . As things have happened in your case," he added. "Fortunately or unfortunately this hypothesis can't be verified experimentally. Rudolf recognizes that he cannot specify the intensity of the electrical current necessary for the mutation; he maintains only that it must exceed a million volts, perhaps even two million. . . . You understand now the interest your case presents."

"I understand," he repeated absently.

"All the information they have had about you — and they have had plenty — confirms the hypothesis. Some members of Goebbels's entourage are enthusiastic. They have made appeals through diplomatic channels, in the name of science, for the good of humanity, etc. Several universities and scientific institutes have invited us for a series of lectures — me, you, Dr. Gavrilă, and anyone else I want to bring; in a word, they want us to lend you to them for a period of time. And because we are reluctant, the Gestapo has been given a free hand. . . ."

He stopped, as though he had suddenly lost his breath. For the first time he seemed tired, aged.

"We had to hand over to them copies of the reports made in the first weeks at the hospital. It's a customary thing to do, and we couldn't refuse. Of course, I haven't informed them of everything. As far as the most recent materials are concerned — among others photostats of your notebook and copies of the recordings — all these were shipped to Paris. Bernard and his coworkers are studying them now, and later they will be deposited at one of the laboratories of the Rockefeller Foundation. . . . But I see you aren't listening anymore," he added, getting to his feet. "You're tired. You'll learn the rest later."

"The rest" seemed interminable. And sometimes it seemed of no interest to him, and at other times it seemed he was hearing things he had learned already, although he could not specify when or under what circumstances. He was amused in particular by the investigations made in connection with the lightning of Easter night. How had it happened that the cloudburst did not extend beyond a certain perimeter, and that only one bolt of lightning had struck — and in a rather unusual way, because the faithful who were waiting in the narthex of the church had seen the lightning as an endless incandescent spear? In any event, along with the specialists sent by Dr. Rudolf, who gathered all sorts of information about the form and intensity of the light in the flash, there came also a famous dilettante, the author of several studies *estruca disciplina*. In less than a week he had succeeded in reconstructing the perimeter covered by the rainfall, and he was now interpreting the symbolism of the space where the bolt had struck.

"But these inquiries and investigations have only an anecdotal value," the Professor continued. "The only serious thing is Dr. Rudolf's decision to begin experiments in electrocution, once he has completed his file by having a few conversations with you."

"But what else could I tell him?" he asked.

"That, no one knows. Perhaps the additional information will be obtained through certain laboratory experiments, by producing, for instance, a series of artificial lightning flashes and hoping you will recognize by the intensity of the light the one that struck you. Perhaps he wants to find out straight from your mouth what you felt at that moment, and why you had the sensation of being sucked up by a fiery cyclone that had burst directly over your head. I don't know. It is suspected, however, that the electrocution experiments will be made on political prisoners. And *that* crime must, at all costs, be avoided."

He had let his moustache grow as he had been told, thick and bushy.

"The modification of your face will take place later," he was told on the evening of September 25.

The Professor could scarcely contain himself. "Chamberlain and Daladier are in Munich," he said as he entered the room. "Anything could happen now, any day. . . . Those who are concerned with you have changed their plan," he began after a pause, taking his usual place in the chair. "You will be evacuated at night, in great secrecy, but in such a way that the others find out, or more precisely, so that they see the car in which you will be transported. Then, twenty or twenty-five kilometers away..."

"I believe I've guessed the rest," he interrupted, smiling. "Twenty or twenty-five kilometers from Bucharest an accident will be staged."

"Exactly. There will even be several witnesses. The press will speak about a routine accident in which three men perished by incineration. But the various wire services will learn that the victims were you and the two agents who were accompanying you, en route to an unknown destination. They will be given to understand that the agents wanted to hide you away in a very safe place...."

"That's the way it will happen," the Professor resumed after a pause. "I don't know where you'll be hidden. But there they will make the modifications of which I spoke. In a month at most, with a regular passport, you will be transported to Geneva — how, I don't know; I wasn't informed. Bernard proposed Geneva. He believes that at the present moment Paris is not the safest place. He will come to see you as soon as possible. I'll come also," he added. "At least, I hope to."

# 3

He never saw the Professor again. At the end of October the older man died. Dominic had been afraid that would happen ever since the day when the Professor had burst into his room saying, "Things are more serious than we expected!" He had had a vision then of the doctor putting his hand to his heart and collapsing, moaning; then he had heard a scream, doors slamming, footsteps rapidly departing on the stairs. Only when the Professor had approached him and asked, "Don't you feel well? Did you have a bad night?" did he return to his senses. But from then on, the vision had kept haunting him. When Dr. Bernard told him, "I have a piece of sad news to give you," he was ready to reply, "I know, the Professor has died."

Dr. Bernard came to see him at least once a month. They would spend almost the whole day together. Sometimes, after listening to him answer certain questions, he would bring the recorder closer and ask him to repeat the answers. Fortunately the questions had to do with memory, the modification of behavior (relations with people, animals, events as compared with his previous way of behaving), his adaptation of his personality to a paradoxical situation (did he believe he could still love someone in the same way he did when he was that age before?), questions to which he could respond without fear. Each time he came, Bernard brought him a sum of money (from a fund put at his disposal by the Rockefeller Foundation, he explained). He had assisted him also in getting a job at the university, entrusting to him the task of coordinating materials for a history of medical psychology.

After the occupation of France, there was a long interval during which he received no news, although, until December 1942, he continued to receive a check each month directly from the Rockefeller Foundation. At the beginning of 1943 a letter arrived from Dr. Bernard, posted in Portugal. It informed him that he would soon write "a long letter, because there is much to tell." But he had received nothing more. Only after the liberation of France, through one of his assistants, did he find out that Dr. Bernard had been killed in an airplane accident in Morocco in February of 1943.

He went each day to the library and asked for many books and collections of old periodicals. He leafed through them attentively, took notes, wrote bibliographical cards; but all this work constituted a camouflage. Once he had read the first few lines he *knew* what would follow. Without understanding the process of anamnesis (as he was accustomed to call it), he discovered that with any text he had before him, if he wanted to find out the content, he immediately *knew* it. Some time after he had begun work at the library he experienced a long, dramatic dream, which he remembered only fragmentarily, however, because he had interrupted it by waking up several times. There was one detail in particular he remembered: in the aftermath of his electrocution, his mental activity anticipated somewhat the condition men will attain some tens of thousands of years hence. The principal characteristic of the new humanity will be the structure of its psycho-mental life: all that has ever been thought or done by men, expressed orally or in writing, will be recoverable through a certain exercise of concentration. In fact, education then will consist in the learning of this method under the direction of instructors.

In short, I'm a "mutant," he said to himself on awakening. I anticipate the post-historic existence of man. Like in a science-fiction novel, he added, smiling with amusement. He made such ironic reflections primarily for the "Powers" that were watching over him. *In a certain sense, what you say is true*, he heard himself thinking. *But in distinction to characters in science-fiction novels, you have retained the freedom to accept or reject this new condition. At the moment you wish, for one reason or another, to return to the other condition, you are free to do it.*

He breathed deeply. "Therefore, I'm free!" he exclaimed after looking around carefully. "I'm free, and yet . . ." But he did not dare continue the thought.

Already in 1939 he had decided to describe his recent experiences in a special notebook. He had begun by commenting on this fact (which, he thought, would confirm the "humanity of post-historic man"): spontaneous knowledge, which in a sense was automatic, did not destroy his interest in research or the joy of discovery. He chose an example easily verified: the pleasure with which a lover of poetry reads a poem he knows almost by heart. He can recite it, yet sometimes he prefers to read it. This is because the new reading gives him the opportunity to discover beauty and meanings that he had not suspected heretofore. It was the same with all that science he received ready-made, all the languages and literatures he had discovered he knew: they had not diminished the joy of learning and investigating.

Reread after several years, some of the sentences fascinated him: "You learn well or with pleasure only that which you know already." "Do not compare me with a computer. Like me, if the computer is correctly 'fed,' it can recite the *Odyssey* or the *Aeneid*, but I recite them *differently* each time." Or, "The blessings that any cultural creation (*n.b.: cultural* creation, not only artistic) can afford are unlimited."

He always remembered with a thrill the mysterious epiphany of the two roses. But from time to time it pleased him to contest the validity of the philosophical argument. There ensued then long dialogues that delighted him. He even promised himself to write them down, primarily for their literary value (which it seemed to him they possessed). The last time, however, the dialogue had ended rather quickly, even abruptly. Basically, he repeated to himself that winter evening in 1944, such parapsychological phenomena can be the effect of forces we do not know, but which can be controlled by the unconscious. *That's very true*, he heard himself thinking. *Every action is effected by a force more or less unknown. But after so many experiences, you ought to revise your philosophical principles. You suspect what I'm referring to.* "Yes, I believe so," he acknowledged, smiling.

Several times during the last years of the War he had discovered that his reserves at the bank were exhausted. Each time he would wait for the solution of the crisis, curious and at the same time impatient. The first time he had received a money order for 1,000 francs from a person of whom he had never heard. His letter of thanks was returned with the indication: "Unknown at this address." Another time he had met by chance one of his colleagues in a restaurant at the train station. On learning that he was going to spend a week at Monte Carlo, he asked him to enter the Casino three days hence at seven P.M. (at *exactly* seven, he insisted) and, at the first table in the first roulette salon, to put 100 francs on a certain number. He requested him to keep the matter secret, and he repeated the request after the young man had returned in great excitement bringing him 3,600 francs.

The last time in particular delighted him. (It was this of which he thought first when he heard, *You suspect what I'm referring to.*) He was passing the three windows of a stamp dealer's shop as he did every time he returned from the library. This time, without understanding why, he stopped and began to look, at random, at the stamps displayed there. Philately had never interested him, and he wondered why he could not pull himself away from one of the windows, apparently the least attractive one. When he set eyes on an old and modest-appearing album, he realized that he *had* to buy it. It cost five francs. At home, he began to thumb through it, attentive, curious, although he did not know what he was seeking. Undoubtedly, it had been a beginner's album, perhaps that of a lycée pupil. Even an amateur like himself realized that the stamps were recent and commonplace. All of a sudden, he took a razor blade and began cutting open the cardboard bindings. He removed several cellophane envelopes, full of old stamps. It was easy to guess what had happened: someone, persecuted by the regime, had succeeded by this device in removing a large number of rare stamps from Germany.

He returned the next day and asked the proprietor of the shop if he remembered who had sold him the album. He did not know: he had bought it in a lot of old albums at an auction several years previously. When he showed him the stamps he had removed from the binders, the dealer paled.

"Such rarities have not been seen for a long time, neither here in Switzerland nor in other countries!" If he were to sell them now, he could obtain at least 100,000 francs. But if he were to wait a while, at any international auction he could obtain as much as 200,000.

"But since I bought them from you for nothing I consider it only fair that I divide the money half and half with you. Right now I need a few thousand francs. The rest of my share, according to how you sell the stamps, you may deposit to my account at the bank."

How such events would have thrilled Leibniz! he said to himself, smiling. To feel yourself obliged to revise your philosophical principles because, because in a mysterious way . . .

Beginning in 1942 he understood that the official version of the accident no longer was accepted either by the Gestapo or by other secret services — which, for various reasons, were interested in his case. Very probably, indiscretions had been made in Bucharest, corroborated later by certain particulars obtained at Paris from the circle of Dr. Bernard's assistants. But if it had been discovered that he was living at Geneva, it was not known what he looked like, and his name was not known. To his surprise, he discovered one evening, when leaving a cafe, that he was being followed. He succeeded in losing the pursuer, and he spent the next week in a village near Lucerne. Soon after he returned to Geneva, the incident was repeated: this time two men dressed in trench coats were waiting for him in front of the library. One of the librarians came down just then; he asked to be allowed to accompany him. After a while, when the librarian could no longer doubt that they were indeed being followed, they caught a taxi. A brother-in-law of the librarian was a functionary of the Bureau of Aliens. From him he learned later that he had been mistaken for a secret agent, and a telephone number was given him that he could call in case of

need. It amused him that although the Gestapo and probably other Services were looking for him, the immediate
risks were due to a confusion with an ordinary informer
or secret agent.

From the first year on, on the advice of Dr. Bernard,
he had kept his books of personal notes in a safety deposit box in the bank. Then he gave up using notebooks;
he wrote instead on a pad that he carried with him at all
times. Certain pages containing too intimate confessions
he deposited at the bank as soon as he had written them.

The same evening he had taken refuge near Lucerne,
he had decided to complete his autobiographical notes:

I am not a clairvoyant or an occultist, nor do I belong to
any secret society. One of the documents in my safety deposit box summarizes my life which began in the spring
of 1938. My first experiences were described and ana-
lyzed in the reports of Professors Roman Stănciulescu
and Gilbert Bernard and sent by the latter, later, to a laboratory of the Rockefeller Foundation. But they concern
only the external aspects of the mutation process set in
motion in April 1938. I mention them nevertheless because they validate in a highly scientific way some of the
things contained in the other documents deposited at
the bank.

I do not doubt that the eventual investigator, beginning to read through the aforementioned documents, will
ask himself the same question that I have asked many
times in the past seven years: Why *me*? Why has this mu-

tation happened to me, of all people? From the short autobiography that will be found in Portfolio A it will be seen clearly that even before being threatened by total amnesia, I had not succeeded in doing any major thing. I was attracted, in my youth, to many sciences and disciplines, but, except for a great deal of reading, I accomplished nothing. So then, why me? I don't know. Perhaps because I had no family. Perhaps I was chosen because as a young man, I wanted to possess a universal education, and then, at the very moment when I was on the verge of losing my memory completely, I was gifted with a universal erudition such as will become accessible to man only many thousands of years from now.

I have written this note because if, contrary to all expectations, I were to disappear now, I want it to be known that I had no merit and no responsibility in the process of mutation that I have described as fully as possible in the notebooks grouped in Portfolio A.

The next day he continued:

For reasons explained in Portfolio B, I was brought to Switzerland and camouflaged in October 1938. That up to today, January 20, 1943, I have not been identified (and eventually captured) might seem incomprehensible. The reader will wonder how I could have passed unobserved for so many years, although I constituted an exceptional case: I was a "mutant" and had access to means of knowledge still inaccessible to mankind. This question I asked myself also, several times, between 1938 and 1939. But I quickly realized that I did not risk betraying myself—and therefore being identified—for the simple reason that in the presence of others I behaved like an average intellectual. In 1938-39 I was afraid I would give myself away conversing with professors and colleagues of mine at the university: I *knew* more than any of them and I *understood* things they never suspected existed. But to my surprise and great relief, I discovered that in the presence of others, *I couldn't make myself appear as I was*, just as an adult, having a conversation with a child, knows that he cannot communicate—and therefore he does not try to communicate—anything but facts and information accessible to the mental capacities of the child. This continuous camouflage of the immense possibilities that have been put at my disposal has not forced me to lead a "double life"; not in the presence of children, nor parents, nor pedagogues have I lived a "double life."

In a sense, my experience has an exemplary value. If someone were to tell me that there exist among us saints or authentic magicians, or Bodhisattvas, or any other kind of person endowed with miraculous powers, I should believe him. By virtue of their very mode of existence such men could not be recognized by the profane.

Beginning with the morning of November 1, 1947 he decided to cease writing notes in French, but to use instead an artificial language that he had constructed with passion, almost as a man possessed, over the past few months.

What fascinated him about it especially was the extraordinary flexibility of the grammar and the infinite possibilities of the vocabulary (he succeeded in introducing into the system of purely etymological proliferation a corrective borrowed from the theory of aggregates). Now he could describe situations that were paradoxical, apparently contradictory, impossible to express in existing languages. The way this linguistic system was constructed, it could be deciphered only by means of a perfected computer; therefore, he estimated, not before 1980. This certainly permitted him to reveal facts that until then he had not dared to confess in writing.

As usual, after a morning devoted to work, he went for a stroll along the shore of the lake. Upon returning he stopped at the Cafe Albert. As soon as he saw him, the waiter brought coffee and a bottle of mineral water. The waiter also brought him the newspapers, but he did not have time to look at them. A tall, distinguished looking man (seemingly emerged from a portrait by Whistler, he thought to himself) stopped in front of him and asked permission to sit at his table. The man was still rather youthful, although the old-fashioned style of his jacket added six or seven years to his appearance.

"It is curious that we should meet on just this day," he said, "a day so important for you. I am Comte de Saint-Germain. At least so I'm told," he added with a wry smile. "But is it not curious that we meet today, the day following the discovery of the Essene manuscripts from the Dead Sea? Surely you have heard . . ."

"Just what the papers have written."

The man looked at him for a moment, then raised his hand. "The same, and without sugar," he ordered.

"All meetings of this sort," he began after the waiter had brought the coffee, "all meetings between incredible people like us have an air of artificiality about them. The consequence of bad literature, pseudo-occultist books," he added. "But we must resign ourselves: nothing can be done about folklore of mediocre quality. The legends that enchant certain contemporaries of ours are in detestably bad taste. I recall a conversation I had with Matila Ghyka in London in the summer of 1940. It was soon after the fall of France. That admirable savant, writer, and philosopher (in parenthesis let me say I value highly not only *Le nombre d'or,* as does everyone, but also his early novel, *La pluie d'étoiles*) — that incomparable Matila Ghyka told me that the Second World War, which at that time had scarcely begun, was in reality an occult conflict between two secret societies, the Templars and the Teutonic Knights. If a man of intelligence and learning could believe that, it is not surprising that occult traditions are treated with contempt.... But I see you aren't saying anything," he added, smiling.

"I'm listening. It's interesting."

"Anyway, there is no need for you to say very much. I shall ask you only, at the end, to answer one question. ... I don't claim to know who you are," he began again after a pause. "But there are several of us who, since 1939, have known about your existence. The fact that you had appeared suddenly and independently of the traditions we knew induced us to believe, on the one hand, that you had a special mission, and on the other hand, that you had access to means of knowledge much superior to those at our disposal. There is no need for you to confirm what I'm saying. I have come to see you today because the discovery of the Essene manuscripts from the Dead Sea is the first sign of a well-known syndrome. There will follow, rather quickly, other discoveries, and with the same significance. . . ."

"Which is — ?" he interrupted, smiling.

The stranger scrutinized him before replying. "I see you are putting me to the test. Perhaps you're right. But the significance of the discoveries is clear: the manuscripts from Qumran reveal the doctrines of the Essenes, a secret community about which almost nothing precise is known. Likewise, the Gnostic manuscripts discovered recently in Egypt and still unstudied will reveal certain esoteric doctrines, ignored for almost 1,800 years. Soon there will follow other similar discoveries disclosing other traditions that have remained secret until our day. The syndrome to which I refer is this: the revelation in series of secret doctrines. The cycle is closed. This I knew long ago, but after Hiroshima I knew also the way it would end."

"Very true," he whispered absently.

"The question I wanted to ask you is this: employing all the knowledge that has been transmitted to you, do you know precisely the way the 'Ark' will be arranged?"

"The ark?" he asked, surprised. "Are you thinking of a replica of Noah's ship?"

The other looked at him again, puzzled and irritated at the same time.

"It's only a metaphor. A metaphor that's become a cliché," he added. "You find it in all the so-called occultist pulp literature. . . . I refer to the transmission of the tradition. The essential is never lost, I know, but I'm thinking of the many other things that, although they do not represent the essential, seem to me nevertheless indispensable to a truly human existence: for instance, the Occidental artistic treasury, above all music and poetry, but also a part of classic philosophy and certain sciences."

"I believe you can imagine what those few survivors of the cataclysm will think about science," he interrupted, smiling. "Probably post-historic man, as I have heard him called, will be allergic to science for at least a century or two!"

"It is very probable," the stranger agreed. "But I was thinking of mathematics. . . . Anyhow, that's what I wanted to ask about."

He sat thinking for a long time, hesitating to reply. "To the extent I understand your question, I can say only that . . ."

"Thank you, I understand!" the other exclaimed, unable to conceal his joy. He bowed low, shook his hand with genuine sincerity, and strode toward the door. It seemed to him, watching the man leave in such haste, that someone must have been waiting for him just outside in the street.

"I signaled to you several times," said the proprietor in a confidential tone, "but you didn't see me. He used to be a regular customer of ours; everyone knows him: Monsieur Olivier, but some say he is a doctor, Dr. Olivier Brisson. For some time he was a school teacher, but one day he left the school and the city without informing anyone in advance. I don't believe he's all there. He strikes up conversations with people and introduces himself as Comte de Saint-Germain."

He remembered that meeting when he observed that, in a curious way, the scenario was beginning to be repeated. That year he became friends with a young Californian, Linda Gray, who among other things had, for him, the great merit of not knowing jealousy.

One evening, unexpectedly, when he had not yet poured their second cups of coffee, she said to him, "I found out that you were a good friend of a famous French doctor...."

"He died," he interrupted her. "He was killed in an airplane accident in the winter of 1943."

The young woman lit a cigarette and after inhaling the first smoke she continued, without looking at him, "Some believe it wasn't an accident. They say the plane crashed because... Actually, I don't understand it very well, but you'll find out all about it when he gets here. I told him to come at 9:00," she added, looking at her watch.

"Who's coming at 9:00?"

"Dr. Monroe. He's the director, or something else important, at the Gerontology Laboratory in New York."

He recognized him immediately. He had seen the man several times at the library and then, just a few days ago, at the cafe. The man had begged leave to sit at his table, and he had no more than sat down when he asked him if he knew Dr. Bernard. "I knew him very well," he had replied. "But I promised never to discuss the history and significance of our friendship."

"Forgive me if I needed to resort to this stratagem," he began, extending his hand. "I'm Dr. Yves Monroe, and I have investigated the materials of Dr. Bernard in New York. As a biologist and gerontologist, I'm interested in one thing in particular: to stop the proliferation of new, dangerous myths — for example, the belief that youth and life can be prolonged in any way other than by the means we use today, that is, purely biochemical ones. Do you know what I'm referring to?"

"No."

"I refer, in the first place, to the method proposed by Dr. Rudolf: electrocution by means of a million or more volts. That's insane!"

"Fortunately, I believe his method was never tried."

The doctor picked up his whiskey glass and began to turn it around absently between his fingers.

"No, it was not," the doctor continued, giving him an icy stare. "But the legend was circulated that Dr. Bernard knew a somewhat analogous case of a rejuvenation induced by the electrical charge from a bolt of lightning. The materials on deposit at the Rockefeller Laboratory are so general and confused, however, that it is impossible to draw any conclusions. Moreover, I was told that part of the recordings were lost; more precisely, they were destroyed by mistake in an attempt to transfer them to perfect phonodiscs. At any rate, to the extent they are usable, the documents recorded by Professor Bernard refer exclusively to the phases of psycho-mental recuperation and reintegration of the patient struck by lightning."

He broke off his monologue and, without having put his glass to his lips, set it carefully back on the table.

"I have permitted myself to force this meeting," he resumed, "in the hope that you could furnish some explanations with regard to a rather obscure question. You have admitted knowing Dr. Bernard well. Recently the rumor has been going around that he had with him the most important documents, in two valises, and that the airplane in which he was to have crossed the Atlantic crashed because of those two valises. It is not known exactly what they contained, but one of the rival services wanted to assure itself, to avoid — how to say? — any risk. Now, do you know anything precise about the contents of those valises?"

He shrugged in confusion. "I believe that only Dr. Bernard's assistants in Paris would be able to explain."

The doctor smiled with some effort, without trying to hide his disappointment.

"The one who remembers declares he knows nothing. While the others claim they have forgotten. . . . I've also read articles by Professor Roman Stănciulescu in *La Presse médicale*. Unfortunately, Stănciulescu died in the fall of 1939. One of the colleagues on a mission in Bucharest wrote me recently that all his efforts to find out more from Professor Stănciulescu's assistants have been fruitless."

He picked up his glass of whiskey again, and after turning it around several times between his fingers, he put it to his lips with great care and began to sip very slowly.

"Through the intervention of Dr. Bernard you had, for some three to four years, a Rockefeller stipend. What was the area of your research?"

"Materials for a history of medical psychology," he replied. "I sent them in 1945 to Dr. Bernard's collaborators in Paris."

"Interesting," he said, suddenly lifting his eyes from the glass and scrutinizing him at length.

That night he returned home wistful, preoccupied. He was not sure that Monroe had guessed his identity. On the other hand, he did not understand who Monroe believed him to be: a personal friend of Bernard? A patient? If, however, Monroe had listened to the recordings made at Geneva in 1938-39, he ought to have recognized his voice.

Linda's question the next day calmed him. "What did the doctor mean when he took me aside last evening and said, 'If he ever tells you he's past seventy, don't believe him!'?"

Several weeks later, in front of a cafe that had recently opened, he heard someone calling to him in Romanian, "Domnul Matei! Domnul Dominic Matei!" He turned his head in fright. A tall youth, blond and bare-headed, was hurrying toward him, trying at the same time to open a briefcase.

"I've learned a little Romanian," he said in an awkward French, "but I don't dare speak it. I knew you were here at Geneva, and with all the photographs I had, it wasn't hard to recognize you."

He rummaged nervously in the briefcase and brought out several photographs, frontal views and profiles, from various angles. They had been taken in the fall of 1938 by the surgeon who had succeeded in modifying his facial features so radically.

"And, for any eventuality," he added, smiling, "I'm also carrying with me in the briefcase your family photo albums. Let's go inside this cafe a moment. You can't imagine how excited I was when I saw you a little while ago! I was afraid that when you heard me call 'Domnul Matei!' you wouldn't turn your head."

"I almost didn't," he replied, smiling. "But, I admit, I was curious."

They sat down at a table and after they had ordered a hot lemonade and a bottle of beer, the stranger began to stare at him in fascination and disbelief.

"A few weeks ago, on January 8, you were eighty years old!" he whispered. "You don't look more than thirty or thirty-two. And you look that old only because you're trying to hide your age. . . ."

"I still don't know with whom I have the pleasure to be speaking."

"Excuse me," he said, after sipping a little from his beer. "I'm still very excited. As bettors at a race track say, I put everything on one horse — and I won! . . . I'm Ted Jones, Jr., correspondent for *Time* magazine. It all began some ten years ago when I read your interview, "Struck by Lightning." I was extremely impressed, even after I found out it was apocryphal. But then came the War, and very few people still remember that interview."

He emptied the glass of beer and asked if he could continue in English and if pipe smoke annoyed him.

"Two years ago, when the famous secret archive of Dr. Rudolf was discovered, people began talking again about your case — of course, to the extent it was known from the materials collected by Dr. Gilbert Bernard. But nothing else was known, not even whether or not you were still alive. Unfortunately, since Dr. Rudolf was a notorious Nazi — and besides, he had committed suicide during the last week of the War — everything having to do with his experiments is suspect."

"What kind of experiments?"

"The electrocution of animals, of mammals in particular. Beginning with 1,200,000 volts, up to two million."

"And with what results?"

He tried to laugh, then refilled his glass with beer. "It's a long story," he began.

It was indeed a long, obscure, and inconclusive tale. The first investigations of Rudolf's archive seemed to indicate that in certain cases the victims had not been killed by the electric shock, but since the experiments were stopped a few months later, the consequences of the electrocution could not be followed. In other cases, a modification of the genetic system appeared to have been indicated. Several investigators apparently interpreted such modifications as the indicator of a mutation. But under somewhat obscure circumstances, a good number of items from the archive — among them the most valuable — had disappeared. At any rate, in the absence of any data relative to experimentation with human beings, the Rudolf dossier was not conclusive. On the other hand, the great majority of American scholars rejected *a priori* the hypothesis of regeneration through electricity.

"You were the only argument, and you still are!" he exclaimed. "It was therefore to be expected that the few materials saved from Professor Bernard would be systematically depreciated and, in some cases, destroyed."

"Do you believe that was the way it happened?" Matei interrupted.

The other hesitated a few moments before replying. "I have strong motives for so believing. Fortunately, I was sent as correspondent to Romania."

Even before going to Romania, he had learned Romanian well enough to be able to read it and go about by himself on the street and in stores. He had the luck to meet and become friends rather quickly with Dr. Gavrilă, in whose possession he found the family album and all the documentation assembled by the Professor.

"What an extraordinary article could be published! 'Man Rejuvenated by Lightning!' With photos, documents, the declarations of Professor Roman Stănciulescu, Dr. Gavrilă, and others who took care of you, with the interview I'm having now, and lots of other pictures taken here in Geneva, in February 1948!"

Jones stopped himself and tried to relight his pipe, then gave it up and looked deeply into his eyes.

"Although your English is perfect, I see that you aren't saying anything."

"I'm waiting for what comes next."

"Good thinking! What I'm about to say is as spectacular and mysterious as your experience. For ethical and political reasons, the article *cannot* be published. Anything that might give rise to confusions, anything that might seem in one way or another to confirm the theory of Dr. Rudolf, must be kept from publication. Especially now when the voting of massive funding for institutes of gerontological research is at stake. . . . Have you nothing to say?"

He shrugged. "I believe everything has happened as it had to happen. I'm sorry about your work and the time you've lost, but the consequences of the article would be disastrous. If men — more precisely, *certain* men — were sure that electrocution could solve the problem of regeneration and rejuvenation, we could expect anything. I believe it's preferable to let biochemists and gerontologists continue their investigations. One day, sooner or later, they'll arrive at the same results."

Jones smoked, watching him drink from his glass of lukewarm lemonade. "In any event," he said presently, "you also must be considered. When we planned the article, we didn't think about what could become of your life after its publication."

"In a way, something's already begun to happen," Matei interrupted good humoredly. "How did it happen that you discovered me so easily? I supposed that Dr. Gavrilă and all the others in Romania believed me dead long ago, killed in an auto accident."

"So they do believe, the majority of them. Dr. Gavrilă believed it too, until I informed him, in great secrecy, that you were alive and living in Geneva. . . . Don't think I found this out from anyone," he added, smiling enigmatically. "I discovered it by myself, when I was told that Dr. Monroe had come to Geneva to discuss certain details with a friend of Professor Bernard. I guessed immediately that that friend could only be you! Of course, obviously, neither Monroe nor any of the others at the Laboratory of Gerontology believe — *nor can they believe* — such a thing."

"That's good news!"

"The truth *will* come out," Jones continued, not trying to hide his satisfaction. "The story's too wonderful to be buried under a pall of silence. I am going to write a novel," he added, beginning to clean his pipe. "In fact, I've already started. For you it presents no danger. The action takes place in Mexico, before and during the war years, and the majority of the characters are Mexicans. Of course, I'll send you a copy of it if, when it appears, you're still on the same terms of friendship with Linda. I knew her brother well; he was a pilot, killed on Okinawa."

He stopped abruptly and, as though he had just remembered something important, he opened the briefcase. "I was about to forget the family photo album," he said. "I promised Dr. Gavrilă that if I was successful in finding you, I'd give it to you. They are precious documents: memories from — how shall I put it? — memories from your first youth!"

Back at his place, he wrapped the album in a sheet of white paper, placed it inside a large envelope, and sealed it. In the upper left-hand corner he wrote: "Received February 20, 1948 from Ted Jones, Jr., correspondent for *Time* magazine in Bucharest. Brought on behalf of Dr. Gavrilă."

Things have become simplified and complicated at the same time, he said to himself, opening his writing pad. He began writing in French, telling about the meeting and summarizing the conversation with Jones. Then he added:

He confirms Dr. Monroe's information: the systematic destruction of the documents from 1938-39. The only reports concerning the process of physiological reconstruction and anamnesis. The only scientific proofs of regeneration and rejuvenation by means of a massive electrical discharge. This means that the *origin* of the phenomenon of mutation no longer matters. *Why?*

He interrupted his writing and remained pensive for some moments.

Obviously, from the autobiographical sketch and from other notes grouped in Portfolios A, B, and C, the eventual reader will be able to learn the essentials. But without the materials collected and annotated by Professors Stănciulescu and Bernard, my testimony has lost its documentary value. Moreover, almost all of my notes refer to the consequences of the anamnesis, in a word, to the experiences of a mutant that anticipate the existence of post-historic man. The Stănciulescu-Bernard documents did *not* contain information relative to those experiences, but, to a certain extent, they ensured their credibility. I can draw but one conclusion: my testimony is addressed to a reader in the near future, let us say in the year 2000. But to whom?

A provisional answer could be this: in the aftermath of nuclear wars that will have taken place, many civilizations, beginning with the Occidental one, will be destroyed. Undoubtedly, the catastrophe will unleash a wave of pessimism heretofore unknown in the history of mankind, a general despondency. Even if all the survivors do not fall prey to the temptation of suicide, very few will still have enough vitality to be able to hope in man and the possibility of a human species superior to *homo sapiens*. Discovered and deciphered then, this testimony could counterbalance the despair and universal wish for extinction. By virtue of the simple fact that they exemplify the mental potential of a humanity that will come to birth in a far-off future, such documents demonstrate, because they anticipate, the reality of post-historic man.

This hypothesis presupposes the preservation of all the material deposited today in the safe-deposit box. I am ignorant as to how this safeguarding will be assured. But, on the other hand, I do not doubt that the material will be preserved. Otherwise, my experience would have no meaning.

He put the pages he had written into another envelope, sealed it, and set off for the bank. As he was locking the door, the telephone began to ring. He could hear it ringing all the way down the stairs.

# 4

The summer of 1955 was an unusually rainy one, and in Ticino thunderstorms occurred daily. Nevertheless, no one remembered having ever seen the sky as black as it was on the afternoon of August 10. When the first flashes of lightning crossed the sky above the city, the power station shut off the current. For almost half an hour lightning bolts fell in rapid succession, as if there were one endless explosion. From the window he watched where the lightning struck, toward the west, on the rocky hills that sprouted up abruptly in the direction of the mountains. The torrential rain gradually abated, and by three the sky had begun to lose its jet-black hue. Soon the street lights were turned on, and, from the window, he could see the street now, all the way to the cathedral. He waited for the rain to stop; then he went downstairs and headed for the police station.

"A little before noon," he began in a neutral, purely informative tone, "two women started out, intending to drive up to Trento. They asked me if I knew a road that was not too winding. I gave them directions, but I advised them to postpone their excursion, because they were in danger of being overtaken by a storm before reaching shelter at Helival. They replied that they were used to mountain storms and that in any event they could not postpone the trip. Their vacation would be over in a few days and they would have to return home."

The policeman listened to him politely, but without showing much interest.

"I don't know them," he continued. "I did hear the older lady addressing the younger: she called her Veronica. I believe I can guess what's happened. When the storm broke out, they were probably on the road that runs under the walls of the mountain, at Vallino, right where most of the lightning struck. I was at the window and I saw them," he added, realizing that the other was looking at him curiously, almost incredulously. "I imagine many rocks were dislodged. I'm afraid they were struck or even buried by the rockslide."

He knew it would not be easy to convince him.

"I can go by myself in a taxi and look for them," he resumed. "But if it happened as I suspect, we could not — the two of us, the driver and I — get them out from under the rocks by ourselves. We would need picks and shovels."

In the end, however, he had to accept that solution. If he needed help, he would telephone from the first service station and the police would send ambulances and everything needed. When he was approaching Vallino, the sky became clear, but here and there rocks were scattered on the highway, and the driver reduced his speed.

"I don't believe they had time to reach the shelter. Probably after the storm broke, they took refuge in one of the crevices in the walls."

"Some of them are as large as the mouth of a cave," observed the driver.

They both saw her at the same moment. Probably she had died of fright when lightning struck a few steps away. She was a woman well along in years, with gray hair cut short. She did not appear to have been killed by falling rocks, although a boulder had come to rest right beside her and had caught a corner of her skirt. Then he thought he heard a moan, and he began to search among the rocks.

"Veronica!" he called out several times.

They both heard a groan, then several short cries, followed by words in an unknown tongue pronounced rapidly, like an incantation. The falling rocks had piled up in front of the niche where Veronica had taken shelter, almost entirely blocking it. If he had not heard her groaning and crying out, he would never have suspected she was buried there. Just above, at a height of over two meters, a fissure opening into the cave could be seen. Scrambling up with difficulty, he saw her and called out her name, gesturing at the same time. The girl looked up, startled yet happy to see him. She tried to stand upright, but although she was not injured the place was too cramped and she could only half rise.

"The police will soon be here," he told her in French.

Then, because the girl looked as if she didn't understand, he repeated himself in German and Italian. Veronica wiped her hand across her cheek several times and started to speak. At first he realized she was speaking in a dialect of Central India, and then he distinguished whole sentences pronounced in Sanskrit. Bending closer to her, he whispered, "*Shanti! Shanti!*" and recited several canonical benedictions. The girl responded with a smile, then held up one hand to him, as though she wanted to show him something.

He stayed there pressed against the cliff, listening to her, trying to calm her and encourage her with familiar Sanskrit expressions until the ambulance and the police wagon arrived. They managed to move the rocks by digging underneath the edge of the slide that was nearest the road. After an hour the girl succeeded in getting out with the help of a rope ladder. At the sight of the police and the van she began to scream in fright. She took Dominic's hand, drawing very close to him.

"She's had a shock," he explained awkwardly, "and I think she's suffering from amnesia."

"But what language is she speaking?" someone in the group asked.

"I suspect it's an Indian dialect," he replied cautiously.

From her identification papers it was learned that she was Veronica Bühler, age twenty-five, a school teacher who lived in Liestal, in the Canton Bâle-Campagne. Her companion was Gertrude Frank, a German national, resident for some years in Freiburg, an administrative functionary in a publishing house. The autopsy confirmed the first assumption: death had been caused by a cardiac arrest.

Since he was the only one who could understand Veronica, and the only one in whose presence she was calm, he spent a considerable time at the clinic. He brought a tape recorder, which he took care to hide. He recorded her voice several hours per day, especially when she was speaking about herself. She asserted that her name was Rupini, daughter of Nagabhata of the Kshatrya class, descended from one of the first families of Magadha to have been converted to Buddhism. Before her twelfth birthday she had decided, with her parents' consent, to consecrate her life to the study of the Abhidharma and had been accepted into a community of *bhikuni* (female ascetics). She had studied Sanskrit grammar, logic, and Mahayana metaphysics. The fact that she had memorized over 50,000 sutras had created for her a prestige not only among the instructors and students at the famous Nalanda University but also among many masters, ascetics, and contemplatives. At the age of forty she had become a disciple of the famous philosopher Chandrakirti. She spent several months in a cave, meditating and copying the works of her master. That was where she was when a storm had broken out and she had heard the lightning strike above her on the mountain. Many large rocks were dislodged and, pouring down like a river of stones, they had blocked the mouth of her cave. She had tried in vain to get out. Then suddenly she had seen him overhead, waving and speaking to her in an unknown language.

He was not sure he had understood everything, and

even what he knew he understood he kept for the most part to himself. To the doctors he said that the young woman believed she was living in Central India twelve centuries ago and insisted she was a Buddhist anchorite. Thanks to sedatives she slept most of the time. Several medical doctors and psychologists from Zurich, Basel, and Geneva came to see her. As was to be expected, the newspapers published articles every day, and the number of foreign correspondents who roamed the clinic and interviewed the doctors grew unceasingly.

Fortunately, the solution that he had had in mind from the beginning was the course finally accepted. On the second day, after listening to a tape recording of her autobiographical confessions, he had sent a long telegram to the Oriental Institute in Rome. Then, on the third day, at the hour specified in the telegram, he had transmitted by telephone certain of the girl's statements. At the same time he informed one of C. G. Jung's closest collaborators. Two days later Professor Tucci came from Rome, accompanied by an assistant from the Institute. For the first time Rupini could discuss at length, in Sanskrit, Madhyamika philosophy and could talk about her master, Chandrakirti. All the conversations were recorded and the assistant translated some passages into English for the benefit of the doctors and reporters. The discussion became delicate whenever Rupini asked exactly what had happened to her, where she was, and why no one understood her although she had tried speaking in several Indian dialects in addition to Sanskrit.

"What do you say to her?" he asked Professor Tucci one evening.

"Of course, I begin always by reminding her of *Maya*, the great sorceress, cosmic illusion. It is not, properly speaking, a dream, I tell her, but it participates in the illusory nature of dreaming because it is a matter of the future, therefore of time; now, time is par excellence unreal. . . . I don't believe I've persuaded her. But fortunately, she's enthusiastic about logic and dialectics, and that's mainly what we discuss."

As soon as he suggested a journey to India, more precisely to the province of Uttar Pradesh, where the cave in which Rupini had meditated was located, Professor Tucci agreed that the Oriental Institute should sponsor the expedition. Thanks to the intervention of Jung, the basic expenses were covered by an American foundation. When they learned of this project, several daily papers offered to pay all incidental costs of the expedition in exchange for exclusive rights to the story. It was almost impossible to avoid publicity, especially since the consent of the director of the clinic had to be obtained, as well as that of the Indian government and the family of Veronica Bühler. But inquiries about her family made at Liestal yielded no results. Veronica had been a resident of the city for just five years. Her friends and colleagues knew nothing about her family. It was learned, however, that she had been born in Egypt, that her parents had been divorced when she was five; that her father, who had remained in Egypt, had remarried and no longer had any contact with her, while her mother, with whom she had never gotten along very well, had established herself in the United States, but the address was not known.

Eventually, the clinic permitted the journey to India, on the condition that the patient be accompanied by one of the doctors who had treated her. It was, naturally, understood that she would be put to sleep before leaving the clinic and would continue to sleep until they reached the vicinity of Gorakhpur.

From Bombay a military airplane transported them to Gorakhpur. Here six carloads of reporters and technicians were waiting, together with an Indian television crew in a large van. They journeyed from there toward the frontier of Nepal, to the region where, according to Rupini's account, the cave in which she was accustomed to meditate would be found. Fortunately, in addition to Matei, a pandit from Uttar Pradesh familiar with the Madhyamika philosophy was at Rupini's side when she awoke. At the insistence of the doctor, all the others had camouflaged themselves among the trees ten meters away. As if she recognized him, she addressed the pandit in a threatening way, asking him several questions but not waiting for a reply. Rather, she set off quickly up one of the paths, looking straight ahead, repeating her favorite benedictions, which she had recited so many times at the clinic. After some twenty minutes of climbing, she began to run, panting. With her arm out-stretched, she pointed to the crest of a large rock resting against the face of the mountain.

"That's it!" she exclaimed.

Then, using both hands, she began to scramble up the cliff with surprising agility. When she reached the spot, she pulled up a stunted shrub, cleaned the area of moss and dead branches, uncovered an opening, and, trembling, put her face to the rock and looked inside. Then she remained motionless.

"She's fainted!" someone exclaimed from below, even before Matei had reached her.

"It's true!" he called back, lifting her head gently.

With difficulty, he brought her down and handed her over to the team of technicians. They carried her on a stretcher to the automobile. She was still unconscious and the car was some ten miles distant when the first charge of dynamite exploded. In less than half an hour they had succeeded in reaching the bottom of the cave by means of a rope ladder. With the help of searchlights they saw the skeleton: it was sitting upright, as if death had overtaken it in a posture of yogic meditation. Alongside, on the gravel, were a clay pot, two wooden platters, and several manuscripts. Only when they touched the manuscripts did they realize that they had turned to dust long ago.

The nurse stopped him outside the door. "She's awake," she said, "but she hasn't opened her eyes. She's afraid. . . ."

He went to her bed and laid his hand gently on her forehead.

"Veronica!" he whispered.

She opened her eyes suddenly and, recognizing him, her face brightened in a way he had never before seen it. Taking his hand, she tried to sit up.

"Who are you?" she asked. "I remember you. We asked directions of you earlier today. . . . But where's Gertrude? Where is she? . . ."

He had known from the first, as had all the others in the group, that it would be impossible to avoid publicity. The Indian television had recorded the most dramatic scenes, and tens of millions of spectators who had listened to her speaking in Sanskrit and a Himalayan dialect saw her in the end declaring in a timid English that her name was Veronica Bühler and that she knew well only two languages, German and French, declaring likewise that she had never tried to learn any Oriental language and, with the exception of a few popular books, she had never read anything about India or Indian culture. As was to be expected, precisely this fact excited the Indian public and, twenty-four hours later, worldwide opinion. For the vast majority of Indian intellectuals a clearer demonstration of the doctrine of the transmigration of the soul could not be found: in an earlier existence, Veronica Bühler had been Rupini.

"But I don't believe in metempsychosis," she whispered, frightened, one evening, taking his hand. "I never existed before! Maybe I was possessed by another spirit," she added, seeking his eyes.

And because he didn't know what to say and hesitated, caressing her hand, Veronica hung her head wearily.

"I'm afraid I'll go mad," she said.

The members of the expedition who remained were staying in one of the most deluxe hotels in India, guests of the Indian government. In order to avoid photographers, reporters, and the boldness of the curious, the whole group took their meals in a dining room reserved exclusively for them, kept well guarded. Every day they visited museums or institutes and met great personalities. For their transportation, limousines were provided, and they were always accompanied by a squad of motorcycle police. Otherwise, they did not dare leave the floor on which they were staying. They dared not even go walking in the corridors. Along with the doctor and the nurse, Dominic and Veronica had tried once, after midnight, to go out, hoping to catch a taxi and take a walk in the streets somewhere far away from the hotel. But a great throng was waiting at the exit. They were forced to return, fleeing under the protection of the police.

"I'm afraid I'll go mad," she repeated as they were leaving the elevator.

The next day he succeeded in having a conversation with an American reporter who had tried in vain to accompany them to Gorakhpur. He promised the reporter a long, exclusive interview and other hitherto unpublished material if he would arrange for them to be transported, incognito, to a Mediterranean island, where he and Veronica could live in seclusion for several months.

"Until the cyclone of television cameras and rotary presses has passed," he added. "In less than a year, things will be forgotten and each of us will be able to return to his own business."

Two weeks later they were installed in a villa built after the war on a hill a few kilometers from La Vallette. But the preparations and the recording of the interview had taken longer than expected, and Veronica had begun to show signs of impatience.

"We've talked so much and about so many things, yet I don't understand the essential thing: the transmigration of the soul."

"I'll explain it when we're finally alone."

She looked at him with unexpected warmth. "Will we ever be alone?" she whispered.

At Delhi she had said to him one evening, "When I opened my eyes and saw you, and when you told me about Gertrude, I realized I was thinking about two things simultaneously. I said to myself that although, very probably, both my parents were still alive, without Gertrude I was an orphan. And yet, at the same time, I was thinking: if I were five or six years older, and if he were to ask me to marry him, I'd accept!"

"I'm eighty-seven," he said in jest, smiling.

Then he had seen her laugh for the first time. "I'd be older than that if I were to add the years Rupini lived! But as I told you, I don't believe in that. I *can't* believe it."

"In a sense, you're right. But, I repeat, only *in a sense*. We'll discuss the problem later."

He avoided discussing it in the interview, contenting

himself with citing classical Indian conceptions, from the *Upanishads* to Gautama Buddha, referring also to several contemporary interpretations, especially to the commentaries of Tucci. He succeeded in preserving his own anonymity; he was a young Orientalist who had recently become friends with Veronica. He succeeded above all in preserving the same face he had begun to construct in August, with the hair combed over the forehead and a thick, blond moustache covering his upper lip.

One evening when they were alone on the terrace, Veronica stepped over to his chaise-longue.

"Now explain it to me. But, above all, explain *how you knew.*"

"I have to begin very far back," he said.

It was not until one evening at the beginning of October that he understood. They were seated beside each other on the sofa, watching the lights of the port above the railing of the terrace. Veronica seemed to be looking at him strangely.

"You want to say something, but you don't dare. What is it?" he asked.

"I've been thinking: seeing us together all the time, and living in the same house, people will think we're in love."

He sought her hand and squeezed it gently.

"But, it's so, Veronica. We are in love, we sleep in the same room, in the same bed."

"Is it true?" she asked in a whisper.

Then she sighed, laid her head on his shoulder, and closed her eyes. A few moments later she raised her head suddenly and, looking at him as though she did not recognize him, she began speaking in a foreign language, one he had never heard before. So, that's what it was! he said to himself. That's why we had to meet. That's why all those things happened. Slowly, without haste, in order not to startle her, he went to the study and got the tape recorder. She continued to speak more and more rapidly, looking at her hands. Then she put her wristwatch to her ear and listened, surprised and happy at the same time. Her face lighted up, as if she were about to laugh. But all of a sudden she came to her senses. Startled, she blinked several times and began rubbing her eyes. She staggered sleepily, dizzily toward the couch, and when he saw her swaying, he caught her in his arms. He carried her into the next room and laid her on the bed, covering her with a shawl.

She awoke after midnight.

"I'm scared!" she whispered. "I had an awful dream!"

"What did you dream?"

"I don't want to remember it! I'm afraid it will scare me again. I was somewhere beside a great river, and someone, a stranger, with a head like a dog mask, was coming toward me. In his hand . . . I don't want to remember!" she repeated, reaching out to embrace him.

From that night on, he never left her alone; he was afraid the paramediumistic attack would recur without warning. Fortunately, the gardener and the two young

Maltese women who took care of the house disappeared every night, right after dinner.

"Tell me more," she would urge him each evening, as soon as they were alone. "Explain it to me! Sometimes I'm sorry I don't remember any of all that Rupini knows."

One evening, returning from the garden, she asked him all of a sudden, "Doesn't it seem odd that they should be waiting for us beside the fence! It's as though they're spying on us."

"I hadn't noticed anyone," he replied. "Where were they?"

She hesitated a few moments, avoiding his eyes. "They were there, by the gate, as though they were spying on us. Two men, dressed oddly. But maybe I was mistaken," she added, bringing her hand to her forehead. "Maybe there wasn't anyone at our gate."

He took her arm and drew her slowly along with him. "I'm afraid you've spent too much time in the sun," he said, helping her lie down on the couch.

A week has past, he said to himself, so this must be the rhythm, hebdomadal. Which means that the whole thing could last a month. But what will happen to us then?

When he was sure she was deeply asleep, he tiptoed to the study and returned with the tape recorder. For some time he heard nothing but the blackbirds outside and her slightly agitated breathing. Then her whole face was illuminated by a broad smile. Very softly she pronounced a few words; then there followed a concentrated, anxious silence as though she were waiting for a response that was delayed or that she did not succeed in hearing. Then she began to speak, softly as if she were talking to herself, repeating certain words several times, with different intonations, but all pervaded by a great sadness. When he saw the first timid teardrops on her cheeks, he shut off the recorder and pushed it under the couch. Then, with great care, he stroked her hand and began to wipe her tears. Later, he carried her in his arms to the bedroom. He remained beside her until she awoke. Setting eyes on him, she grasped his hand and squeezed it tightly.

"I was dreaming," she said. "It was a very beautiful dream, but very sad. There were two young people like us, who loved each other and yet couldn't remain together. I don't understand why, but they weren't allowed to stay together."

He was not mistaken: the rhythm was indeed hebdomadal, although the paramediumistic ecstasies (as he had decided to call them) occurred at various hours. Materials for the documentary history of language, he said to himself, classifying the four cassettes. After Egyptian and Ugaritic, there had followed, probably, a sample of Protoelamite and one of Sumerian. We are descending deeper and deeper into the past. Documents for the Ark, he added, smiling. What wouldn't linguists give if they could study them now! But how far back will we go? To the inarticulate protolanguage? And then . . .?

In the middle of December the strangest experience occurred. Fortunately it happened a little before midnight and he had not yet fallen asleep. Veronica burst into a series of guttural, pre-human cries that at the same time exasperated and embarrassed him. It seemed to him that such a regression into animality ought to be attempted only with volunteers, not with an unconscious subject. But, after several moments, there followed groups of clear phonemes with vowels, of an infinite variety, interspersed with short, labial explosions such as he would not have believed possible for a European to reproduce. After half an hour Veronica fell asleep, sighing. Farther than this I don't believe they will go, he said to himself, switching off the recorder. Then he waited. He wanted to be wide awake beside her when she roused from her slumber. Toward morning, however, he fell asleep.

When he awoke, a little before eight, Veronica was still sleeping and he didn't have the heart to wake her. She slept until almost eleven. Discovering how late it was, she sprang frightened from the bed.

"What's wrong with me?" she cried.

"Nothing. Probably you were very tired. And perhaps you had a bad dream."

"No. I dreamed nothing. At any rate, I don't remember dreaming anything."

They decided to spend Christmas Eve and New Year's Eve at a famous restaurant in La Vallette. Veronica reserved a table under the names of Monsieur and Madame Gerald Verneuil. She invented the names and also selected the costumes for New Year's Eve.

"I don't believe we're in danger of being recognized,"

she said. "Even if our pictures appeared last fall on the front pages of all the popular magazines."

"You can be sure they *did* appear," he interrupted her, "and perhaps they're still appearing."

She started to laugh somewhat timidly and yet happily. "I'd like to see them," she said. "The photos in the magazines, I mean. I'd like to have a few as souvenirs. But maybe it's too risky to search for them."

"I'll look around," he volunteered.

But although he searched through many kiosks and bookstores, he found only one magazine, an Italian one, with three pictures of Veronica, all taken in India.

"I seemed younger and better looking then, three months ago," she observed.

A few weeks later he realized she was right. For some time she had not looked so youthful. The documents for the Ark are to blame, he said to himself. The paramediumistic ecstasies have exhausted her.

"I feel tired all the time," she admitted one morning, "and I don't understand why. I do absolutely nothing, and yet I feel tired."

At the beginning of February he succeeded in persuading her to consult a doctor in La Vallette. They waited, then, uneasily for the results of the numerous tests.

"Madame is not suffering from anything, anything at all," the doctor assured him when they were alone. "I have, however, prescribed a series of shots with vitamins and minerals. . . . Perhaps it's the nervous condition that precedes the climacteric in certain women."

"What age do you take her to be?"

The doctor blushed, and rubbed his hands together awkwardly. "Around forty," he said at length, avoiding his eyes.

"And yet, I assure you that she didn't lie to you when she told you she was not yet twenty-six."

The effect of the injections fell short of expectations. Each day she felt more tired; often, after she had been looking in the mirror, he would catch her crying. Once, when he was walking to the park, he heard footsteps coming up quickly behind him, and he turned his head.

"*Professore*," whispered the cook in fright, "*la signora ha il malocchio!*"

I ought to have understood this from the beginning, he told himself. We both have done our duty, and now we must separate. And since a more convincing argument could not be found — aside from a fatal accident or a suicide — this way was chosen: a process of galloping senescence.

He did not dare to tell her, however, until the morning when she showed him her hair: it had turned gray overnight. She wept, leaning against the wall, her face buried in her hands. He knelt beside her.

"Veronica," he began, "I'm to blame for this. Listen to me and don't interrupt. If I continue to live with you, by fall you will have perished! . . . I can't tell you more, I don't have the right. But I assure you that, in reality, you *haven't aged!* Once I disappear from your life, your youth and beauty will return."

Veronica sought his hand in fear, clasped it between hers, and began to kiss it. "Don't leave me!" she whispered.

"Listen to me, I implore you! Listen to me for two or three more minutes. I have been fated to lose all that I love. But I prefer to lose you young and beautiful, the way you were — and will be again, without me — than to see you perishing in my arms. . . . Listen! I'm going to leave, and if in three or four months you don't find yourself as you were last autumn, I shall return. The minute I receive your telegram, I'll come back. I ask just this much: wait three or four months, somewhere far away from me!"

The next day, in a long letter, he explained why he would no longer have a right to live with her once she had regained her youth. And because Veronica seemed to have begun to be persuaded to try the experiment, they decided to leave the villa. She would spend the first few weeks in a rest house run by nuns, and he would take a plane for Geneva.

Three months later he received a telegram: "You were right. I will love you all my life. Veronica." He replied, "You will be happy. Good-bye."

That same week he left for Ireland.

# 5

Without his blond moustache and the bangs that had made him resemble certain poets from the twilight of Romanticism, he was not afraid of being recognized by anyone. Besides, after returning from Malta he frequented other *milieux*, primarily circles of linguists and literary critics. Sometimes, in the course of discussions, the case of Veronica-Rupini came up; judging by the questions he asked, it was quickly understood how little, and how badly, he was informed. In the summer of 1956 he agreed to contribute to a James Joyce documentary album. He accepted because the project allowed him to visit Dublin, one of the few cities he wanted to know. He returned there each year, a little before Christmas or at the beginning of summer.

Not until the fifth trip, in June 1960, did he meet Colomban. He met him by chance one evening when entering a pub off O'Connell Street. When he saw him, Colomban headed straight for him, took his hand between his own hands, and pressed it warmly. Then he invited him to sit at his table.

"How long I've been waiting for you!" he exclaimed pathetically, almost theatrically. "This is the fifth time I've come here, expressly to meet you."

He was a man of indefinite age, freckled, half-bald, with copper-colored sideburns contrasting with the pale blond of his hair.

"If I were to say that I know you, that I know *very well* who you are, you wouldn't believe me. So I shall say nothing. But since I too am probably condemned to live to be a hundred, I want to ask you just this: *What do we do with Time*? I'll explain immediately."

He was gazing at him in silence, smiling, when Colomban suddenly rose from the table.

"Or better, let's ask Stephens," he added, heading toward the bar.

He returned with a young man, thin and carelessly dressed. The youth shook his hand timidly, then sat down opposite him at the table.

"You must forgive his little manias," he said, pronouncing the words slowly. "He asks me all the time to declaim — he believes, perhaps, that I have better diction — to declaim: 'What do we do with Time?' His great discovery would be this, that the question, 'What do we do with Time?' expresses the supreme ambiguity of the human condition. Because, on the one hand, men — *all men*! — want to live long, to exceed, if possible, a hundred years; but in the vast majority of cases, once they reach the age of sixty or sixty-five and retire, *i.e.*, become *free to do what they want*, they become bored. They discover they have nothing to do with their free time. And on the other hand, the older a man becomes the more the rhythm of interior time accelerates, so that those persons — those very few — who *would* know what to do with free time, do not succeed in doing much of importance. . . . Finally, add to it the fact that. . ."

Colomban interrupted him, laying a hand on his arm. "Enough for today. Another day you will say it better, more convincingly."

Then, turning to the other, he added, "We shall return to the problem of Time. Meanwhile, I will ask if this article has come to your attention?"

He handed him a page from an American magazine:

. . . He spoke sometimes of a new quality of life, insisting that it could be, and *must* be, discovered by everyone. The moment he awoke he discovered a great joy that he did not know how to describe; it was, undoubtedly, the joy of feeling himself alive, whole, and healthy, but it was something more: the joy that other people exist, that there are different seasons and that no day is just like any other, the joy that he could see animals and flowers, that he could touch trees. On the street, even without returning the glances of others, he sensed that he was participating in an immense community, that he was a part of the world. Even ugly things — a vacant lot littered with garbage and refuse —were in some mysterious way seemingly illumined by an inner incandescence.

"Very interesting," he said, reaching the end of the column. "But there must be more."

"Certainly there is. It's a whole article, rather long, entitled: 'The Young Man of Seventy.' The author is Linda Gray."

He did not try to hide his surprise. "I didn't know she'd taken up writing," he said, smiling.

"She's been writing a long time, and she writes very well," continued Colomban. "But I wanted to be sure that we are in agreement: longevity becomes bearable, and even interesting, *only* if a technique for simple bliss has been discovered beforehand."

"I don't believe it *is* a matter of a technique," he interrupted amiably.

"With all due respect, I beg to differ with you. Do you know any examples of centenarians or quasi-centenarians who live the bliss described by Linda Gray, other than Taoist solitaries, Zen masters, or certain yogis and certain Christian monks? That is, in a word, practitioners of various spiritual disciplines?"

"Plenty of examples are known. Naturally, the majority are peasants, shepherds, fishermen — 'simple folk,' as they are called. They employ no technique, properly speaking. But, obviously, they practice a certain spiritual discipline: prayer, meditation. . . ."

He stopped speaking abruptly, seeing that someone had stopped at their table, a man well along in years, completely bald, smoking from a long cigarette holder made of amber.

"Your discussion's futile," the man said, addressing Colomban. "In both cases, the problem is the same: without that new quality of life of which Linda Gray speaks, longevity is a burden, and perhaps even a curse, and in that case, *what do we do*?"

"This is Dr. Griffith," Colomban said, introducing him. "He was there with us also when it happened."

He interrupted himself and sought his guest's eyes. "Perhaps it would be better if we explain to him what this is all about," he said to the others.

The doctor sat down and continued smoking intently, with his eyes riveted on one of the yellowing chromolithographs on the wall.

"Tell him," he said after a pause. "But begin with the essential. The essential being," he specified, "not Bran's biography, but the significance of the centenary."

Colomban raised both his arms, as if he wanted to interrupt him and cheer him at the same time.

"If you say one more word, Doctor, you'll have to begin with the end."

Then he turned to look at Matei in what seemed to the latter a somewhat provocative way.

"Although you have the reputation of being omniscient, I'm sure you don't know anything about Sean Bran. Even here in Dublin, few still remember him. He was a poet and at the same time a magician and a revolutionary — or rather, an irredentist. He died in 1825, and, thirty years later, in June 1855, his admirers — he still had, at that time, a good number of admirers — set up, in a square, a monument in his honor: a rather mediocre bust, having for its base a rock from the sea. On the same day they planted an oak tree, some three meters behind the statue."

"It was on June 23," Dr. Griffith specified.

"Correct. And five years ago we, the last admirers of the *poet* and *magician* Sean Bran, organized a ceremony in the square that bears his name. We hoped that as a result of this event there would be renewed interest in Bran's work. We were dreaming, because the few of us who prize his poetry today are not at all in sympathy with his magical ideas and practices, whereas the political activists, those who admire his irredentism. . . ."

"You've forgotten the essential," the doctor interrupted. "You forgot about James Joyce."

"That's very important," said Stephens.

"True," Colomban acknowledged. "If the hopes that we linked to *Finnegans Wake* had been fulfilled, Sean Bran would be a famous name today. Because, as you know," he added, seeking his eyes again, "everything that touches the life or work of the Great Man is destined for fame. An oral tradition, whose origin we have not succeeded in identifying, claims that Joyce in *Finnegans Wake* made many allusions to the aesthetics and above all to the *magical concepts* of Bran. This tradition asserts that Joyce refused to specify more or to indicate the context or even the pages where those allusions are located. For years several of us have labored to discover them: so far, without success. If the tradition is authentic, the allusions lie hidden in those 189 pages of *Finnegans Wake* that still await decipherment."

"Only after it had become necessary for us to admit this failure," Dr. Griffith interrupted, "did we decide to celebrate the centenary. Perhaps we made a mistake in choosing not a commemoration of a biographical nature, but the *centenary of a statue.*"

"At any rate," continued Colomban, "when we gathered in the square, we almost expected an irremediable fiasco. The morning had been torrid. . . ."

"It was the twenty-third of June," specified Dr. Griffith.

"Torrid," repeated Colomban, "and now, at the beginning of the afternoon, the sky was like lead. Even those few reporters who had promised us their support did not dare to remain. The smattering of spectators began to leave as soon as they heard the first thunder and felt the first drops of rain. When the storm broke no one was left but we six, the ones who had taken the initiative in holding the commemoration."

The doctor stood up suddenly. "I believe it's time we started for the square," he said. "It's not far."

"Still, if a taxi comes our way, we'll take it," Colomban added.

They found one before they reached the end of the block.

"So, there were only the six of us left," Colomban continued. "And because it was raining bucketsful, we took refuge under the oak."

"And of course, at a certain moment," he interrupted him, smiling, "at a certain moment..."

"Yes. At a certain moment — when, moreover, we weren't expecting it, because we thought the storm had almost passed, and we were wondering whether we should read the speeches we had in our pockets or whether we should wait for it to clear up in the hope that at least some of the guests would return."

"Yes," Dr. Griffith interrupted, "at a certain moment lightning struck the tree, setting it on fire from top to bottom."

"And yet, it wasn't burned up entirely," Colomban resumed. "Because, as you see," he added after paying the driver and getting out of the cab, "a part of the trunk still remains."

They took several steps forward and stopped at the iron railing surrounding the monument. It was not illuminated, but in the light of the street lamps on the square it could be seen rather well. The rock was impressive the way it stuck up obliquely from the ground, and the bust had acquired a noble, almost melancholic patina. Behind was profiled the thick, mutilated trunk of the oak. One could distinguish the greater portion, burned black, as well as a few timid green branches.

"But why have they left it this way?" he asked. "Why haven't they dug it out and planted another?"

Colomban broke into a short, ironic laugh and began to rub his sideburns nervously. "For the time being, the City considers it — the oak, I mean — an historic monument. Sean Bran has not become popular, but the story of the oak, the oak struck exactly on the centenary of the day it was planted, has been heard all over."

They walked slowly around the fence.

"Now you understand," Colomban resumed, "why the problem of Time interests us. It is said, and I'm convinced it's true — my father knew several cases — it is said that those who take shelter under a tree and escape safe and sound when the tree is struck by lightning are destined to live a hundred years."

"I didn't know before that such a belief existed," he said, "but it seems logical."

It was such an impressive spectacle — the marine rock viewed from behind, with that trunk three meters in diameter, peeled, charred, and yet preserving a few living branches — that he asked permission to go back and look at it again.

"Even more curious," the doctor began a little later when they had returned to the front of the statue again, "curious and yet also sad, is the fact that the next day the police discovered a charge of dynamite hidden under the rock's pedestal. If it hadn't rained, it would have exploded during the speeches and destroyed the statue, or at least mutilated it."

On hearing this, Matei stopped walking and sought the speaker's eyes.

"But why?" he asked, lowering his voice. "Who would have been interested in destroying a historic monument?"

Dr. Griffith and Colomban exchanged knowing glances.

"Many," replied Stephens. "First of all, the irredentists, indignant that the revolutionary Bran was being claimed and honored by a few poets, philosophers, and occultists."

"In the second place," continued Colomban, "the church, more precisely the Ultramontanists and obscurantists who see in Bran the prototype of the satanic magician — which is absurd, because Bran follows the Renaissance magical tradition, the conception of Pico or of G. B. Porta...."

"No need to go into detail," Griffith broke in. "What's certain is that the ecclesiastical hierarchy is not disposed to accept him."

All four of them were now walking in the middle of the deserted, dimly lit street.

"But," Colomban resumed, "to return to the essential, that is, to our problem: condemned to live a hundred years, what do we do with Time?"

"I'd prefer to discuss this another time," Matei interrupted. "Tomorrow, if you wish, or the day after. Suppose we meet toward evening in a public garden or a park."

He had agreed to meet them again because above all he wanted to find out who Colomban thought he was. At a certain moment he had addressed him as if he considered him a specialist on *Finnegans Wake*. On the other hand, he had saved that page from "A Young Man of Seventy" and he knew who Linda Gray was (he knew the prestige she had acquired as an author).

Stephens escorted him all the way to his hotel. As they were about to separate, after looking all around several times, Stephens said, " 'Colomban' is a pseudonym. And it's better that you know — he practices black magic, he and Dr. Griffith. Ask them what happened to the other three who were with them under the oak tree when the lightning struck! And ask them about the title of the book they're writing in collaboration. . . . No, I'll tell you: *The Theology and Demonology of Electricity*."

He liked the title. He set it down in his private notebook after he had summarized the first meeting and tried to specify the significance of the incident of June 23, 1955. He was intrigued by the fact that the explosion which, for political motives, was to have blown up the statue, had been prevented by the rain and replaced by a bolt of lightning that set fire to the centennial oak. The presence of the dynamite constituted an element characteristic of our contemporary era. From that point of view, the incident looked like a parody, almost a caricature, of the epiphany of lightning. And yet the substitution of the object — the tree instead of the statue — remained enigmatic. But nothing he learned in the three meetings that followed contributed to clarifying the problem.

He was reminded of the title four years later, in the summer of 1964, when, at a colloquium on Jung's *Mysterium Conjuctionis*, a young man interjected into the discussion the expression, the "eschatology of electricity." He began by recalling the union of opposites in a single totality, the psychological process which, he said, must be interpreted in the light of Indian and Chinese philosophy. For Vedanta as well as for Taoism, opposites are annulled if they are viewed from a certain perspective, good and evil lose their meaning, and, in the Absolute, being coincides with non-being. "But, what no one dares to say," continued the young man, "is that, in the horizon of these philosophies, atomic wars must be, if not justified, at least accepted."

"I, however," he added, "go even further: I justify nuclear conflagrations in the name of the eschatology of electricity!"

The tumult that erupted in the hall obliged the chairman to withdraw the privilege of the floor from him. A few minutes later, the young man left the room. Matei followed him and caught up with him on the street.

"I regret you were kept from expressing your views fully. Personally, I'm very interested in the idea of the 'eschatology of electricity.' What were you referring to exactly?"

The young man looked him over in disbelief, then shrugged. "I'm not in much of a mood for discussion now," he said. "The cowardice of contemporary thought exasperates me. I'd rather have a beer."

"With your permission, I'll join you."

They sat down on the terrace of a cafe. The younger man did not attempt to hide his irritation.

"Probably, I'm the last optimist in Europe," he began. "Like everyone else, I know what's in store for us: hydrogen, cobalt, and so on. But unlike the others, I try to find a meaning in this imminent catastrophe, and thereby reconcile myself with it, as the old man Hegel taught us. The true meaning of the nuclear catastrophe can only be this: the mutation of the human species, the appearance of the superman. I know, atomic wars will destroy populations and civilizations and will reduce a part of the planet to a desert. But this is the price that must be paid if we are to radically liquidate the past and form a new species, infinitely superior to the man of today. Only an enormous quantity of electricity, discharged over a period of several minutes or hours, could modify the psychomental structure of the unfortunate *homo sapiens* that up to now has dominated history. Taking account of the unlimited potential of post-historic man, the reconstruction of a planetary civilization could be achieved in record time. Of course, only a few million individuals will survive. But they will constitute so many million supermen. Therefore, I use the expression the eschatology of electricity; both the *end* and the *salvation of man* will be obtained by means of electricity."

He stopped speaking and, without looking up, drained his glass of beer.

"But why are you so sure that the electricity discharged by nuclear explosions will force a mutation of a superior order? It might just as well provoke a regression of the species."

The young man jerked his head around and gave him a severe, almost furious look.

"I'm not *sure*, but I *want* to believe it will be that way!

Otherwise, neither the life nor the history of man would have any meaning. I'd be forced then to accept the idea of cosmic and historical cycles, the myth of eternal repetition.... On the other hand, my hypothesis is not only the result of despair; it's based on fact. Have you by chance heard of the experiments of a German savant, Dr. Rudolf?"

"By chance, I have heard. But his experiments, the electrocution of animals, are not conclusive."

"So they say," the young man interrupted him. "But since the Rudolf archive disappeared almost in its entirety, it's hard to judge. At any rate, during the time that that secret archive could be consulted, no indication was found of biological regression. On the other hand, you have read, surely, the novel by Ted Jones, *Rejuvenation by Lightning.*"

"No. I didn't know it existed."

"If the problem interests you, you ought to read it. In an afterword, the author leaves the impression that the novel was based on facts; only the nationality and names of the characters were changed."

"And just what is this novel about?" he asked, smiling.

"Jones describes the regeneration and rejuvenation of an old man who was struck by lightning. A significant detail: the lightning struck in the center of the cranial cap. At eighty years of age the character — who, I repeat, is real — does not look more than thirty. Therefore, we are sure at least of one thing: that in certain cases, electricity in massive doses provokes a total regeneration of the human body, hence a rejuvenation. Unfortunately, concerning the modification of the psychomental experience the novel gives no precise indications; it only makes allusions to hypermnesia. But you can imagine what radical transformations will be brought by the electricity discharged by several dozens or hundreds of hydrogen bombs."

When Matei rose from the table and thanked him, the young man looked at him for the first time with interest, almost with sympathy. On reaching home, he wrote in his pocket notebook: "July 18, 1964. The eschatology of electricity. I believe that I can add: *The End.* I doubt I shall have occasion to record other events or meetings of equal interest."

And yet, in spite of this, two years later, on the tenth of October 1966, he wrote: "Evacuation of the materials. I receive a new passport." Normally, he would have related these two episodes in detail. Especially the admirable (and mysterious) transfer of the materials. He had received through the bank a letter from an air transport firm advising him that the expenses for the transportation of the boxes of manuscripts and tape recordings had already been paid at a branch in Honduras. In accordance with a previous understanding, one of the employees of the bank in Geneva would come to Matei's residence to supervise the packing of the materials. He was, certainly, a specialist and had been informed of the nature of the objects to be packed. After two large boxes, almost full, had been delivered from the bank, both of them worked until almost sunset. With the exception of the private notebooks and a few personal items, everything was packed in bags and boxes, sealed, and numbered. For some time he feared that the evacuation of the materials might indicate an imminent catastrophe, but a consecutive series of dreams reassured him.

Then, although they were succinct and enigmatic, the notes increased in number and frequency. December 1966: "I shall have to write him and thank him. The book is more intelligent than I expected." This referred to the novel that Jones had sent him. He started to add, "Even more extraordinary, how has he guessed my name and found my address?" but he decided against it. February 1967: "Inquiry in connection with the destruction of the Dr. Rudolf archive." In April: "Met R. A. by accident. He tells me in great secrecy that the preliminary investigations have been concluded. He is certain now that Dr. Bernard was carrying in the two valises the most valuable documents (I suspect: The recordings and photostats of the reports of the Professor, and the notebooks of 1938-39)."

On June 3, 1967 he noted: "In India the polemics regarding Rupini-Veronica have begun again. An increasingly large number of savants doubt the authenticity of the recordings made at the clinic. The decisive argument: Veronica and her companion disappeared without trace a little while after the return of the expedition to Delhi. 'Now that almost twelve years have passed,' writes a great materialist philosopher, 'any confrontation with the witnesses has become impossible.' " On October 12: "Linda received the Pulitzer Prize for her book, *A Biography*. Whose?"

Then, on June 12, 1968: "Veronica. Fortunately, she did not see me." After a few moments he added: "In the railway station at Montreux, with two beautiful children by her side, explaining to them a tourist advertising poster. She looked her age, perhaps even somewhat younger. The only thing that matters: she is happy."

On January 8, 1968 he celebrated his one-hundredth birthday in a sumptuous restaurant in Nice, in the company of a young Swedish woman, Selma Eklund, whom he admired for her intelligent and original interpretation of Medieval drama. That same month Selma would be twenty-eight, and he avowed, half in jest, that he was almost forty. But the evening was a failure; probably she was not accustomed to champagne, and before dessert he had to take her back to her hotel. He spent the rest of the evening until after midnight walking on little frequented streets.

He wanted, nevertheless, to mark his "first centennial" (as he liked to call it) by taking a spectacular trip. Many years before, he had been to Mexico, and later to Scandinavia. He wanted now to visit China or Java. But he did not rush to make his decision. I have the whole year at my disposal, he repeated to himself.

One autumn evening he returned home earlier than usual. A hard, chilling rain had forced him to give up his long stroll through the park. He wanted to telephone a girlfriend, but changed his mind, and went to the record cabinet. For a cold night like this, only music . . . Only music, he repeated absently, surprised to find, lost among the records, the family photo album. He pulled it out, frowning. All at once, he felt a chill come over him, as though someone had just opened the window. For a few moments he hesitated, holding the album. *And the third rose?* he heard himself thinking. *Where do you want me to put it? Lay the album down, and show me where you want the rose put. The third rose.*

Baffled, he began to laugh bitterly. I am after all a free man, he said to himself, sitting down in the easy chair. Very carefully and with much excitement he opened the album. A freshly picked rose, maybe such as he had seen but once before, was there in the middle of the page. Happy, he picked it up. He would never have believed a single rose could perfume a whole room. For a long while he hesitated, then he placed it beside him, on the arm of the chair. His eyes came to rest on the first photograph. It was pale, faded, blurred, but he recognized without difficulty his parents' house in Piatra Neamţ.

# 6

It had begun snowing several hours earlier; then, just past Bacău a blizzard was unleashed; but as the train was entering the station the snow ceased to fall, and in a clear blue sky there rose, twinkling, the first stars. He recognized the square, immaculate beneath the fresh snow, although on all sides stood recently constructed apartment houses. And yet it seemed strange that a few days before Christmas there were so few windows lighted. He stood a long while holding his valise, looking with deep emotion at the boulevard that stretched before him. He came to his senses at the moment when the family with whom he had shared the compartment engaged the last taxi. But the hotel where he had reserved a room was rather close. Turning up the collar of his coat, he crossed the square without haste and set off down the boulevard. Only after reaching his destination did he realize his left arm had become stiff. The valise was heavier than he had supposed. He presented his passport and the receipt of the Office of Tourism.

"You speak Romanian very well," remarked the woman at the reception desk after she had examined his passport. She had gray hair, and was wearing eyeglasses without rims. Her distinguished face and the quality of her voice impressed him.

"I'm a linguist," he explained. "I have specialized in the study of Romance languages. And I've been to Romania before. I've even been to Piatra Neamţ. I was a student. . . . By the way, does the Cafe Select still exist?"

"How could it not exist! It's an historic monument. Calistrat Hogaş frequented it — probably you've heard of him."

"Of course!"

"He frequented it from 1869 to 1886, the whole time he was professor here at Piatra Neamţ. They say he liked it . . . . You have Room 19, on the third floor. Take the elevator."

"I believe I'll go first to the Select. It isn't far. I'll be back in an hour, an hour and a half."

It seemed to him that the woman was looking at him in wonderment over her spectacles.

"Don't catch cold," she warned. "The streets are still clogged with snow and more snow is forecast."

Ten minutes later he was convinced the woman was right: certain streets were indeed clogged and he made his way with difficulty. But in the vicinity of the cafe the sidewalk had been cleared of snow and he walked faster. Outside the door he stopped to catch his breath and calm the beating of his heart. On entering he recognized the smell of beer, of freshly ground coffee, and of cheap cigarette smoke. He headed for the back room, where he and his friends used to gather. The room was almost empty; there were just three men at a table, finishing tankards of beer. That explains why they have only one bulb, the weakest one, lighted on the ceiling — to save electricity. He sat down on the couch next to the wall and stared vacantly. As he waited for the waiter, he did not know whether he would ask for a mug of beer or a bottle of mineral water and a cup of coffee. Soon the three rose noisily from their chairs, preparing to leave.

"We haven't arrived at any conclusion again this time," exclaimed one of them, wrapping a woolen shawl around his neck.

"It doesn't matter!" said the second.

"It doesn't matter!" echoed the third, laughing and looking at the other two knowingly. "You know what I mean," he added.

Alone, he wondered if it was worthwhile waiting for the waiter any longer, when it seemed that someone was approaching him timidly, hesitantly, looking at him curiously. Only when he stopped in front of him did he recognize who it was: Vaian.

"It is you, Cucoane Dominic?" exclaimed Vaian, taking his hand with both of his own hands and shaking it over and over. "Praise God, you've returned! You've returned!"

Then he turned his head and called out, "Doctor! Come quickly. He's back! Cuconul Dominic!"

He was still squeezing his hand, pumping it. A few

moments later the whole group invaded the room, with Dr. Neculache in front and Nicodim holding a bottle of Cotnar in his left hand and a half-full glass in his right. They all looked at him closely, repeating his name, exclaiming. He was so moved that he was afraid he would soon feel tears on his cheeks, but with an effort he managed to laugh.

"In other words," he said, "the story begins all over again, from the beginning. I'm dreaming, and when I wake up, it will seem I've just started to dream indeed! Like that story of Chuang-tze and the butterfly."

"Chuang-tze?" Vaian repeated in a whisper. "The story about Chuang-tze and the butterfly?"

"I've told it to you many times," he interrupted, suddenly very well disposed.

Then he heard a voice in the back say, "Send someone to tell Veta!"

"Leave Veta in peace!" he exclaimed. "I'll believe you without Veta. I realize very well I'm dreaming, and that in a minute or two I'll wake up."

"Don't tire yourself, Cucoane Dominic," the doctor spoke up, approaching and laying a hand on his arm. "You've been through a great deal. Don't tire yourself."

He started laughing again. "I know," he began, seemingly trying not to become angry. "I know that all this, our meeting here and all that will follow — all this could have happened really in December 1938."

"But that is when it *is* happening, Cucoane Dominic," Vaian interrupted. "This is December 20, 1938."

"I don't dare tell you what year we are living in, we who are outside this dream. If I were to make the effort I'd wake up."

"You *are* awake, Cucoane Dominic," the doctor said gently. "But you're tired. In fact, you look very tired."

"All right!" he exclaimed suddenly, losing his temper. "Between December 20, 1938 and this evening, many things have happened. The Second World War, for example. Have you heard of Hiroshima? Of Buchenwald?"

"The Second World War?" asked someone in the back. "It's coming, all right; coming fast!"

"Many things have happened since you disappeared and gave us no sign of life," Nicodim began. "Your house has been opened more than once. Books were taken from your library."

"I know, I know!" he interrupted, raising his arm. "I told them what books to look for and bring to me. But that was long ago, long ago."

He was beginning to be irritated by the fact that he could not wake up, even though he knew he was dreaming and he wanted to awaken.

"We've looked all over for you," he heard a familiar voice saying. "The doctor looked for you in several hospitals."

"We heard you'd gone to Bucharest," said Neculache, "and that you were mistaken for someone else there."

"That's what happened," he interrupted. "I was taken for someone else because I was rejuvenated."

He hesitated a moment, then continued triumphantly yet enigmatically.

"Now I can tell you the truth. After the lightning struck me — struck me right on the top of my head — I was rejuvenated. I looked twenty-five to thirty, and after that I didn't change. For thirty years, I've looked the same age."

He noticed how the others were staring at him, and, exasperated, he raised his arms, trying to laugh.

"I know you can't believe it. But if I were to tell you how many other things happened, all on account of the lightning, how many Oriental languages I have learned — that is, I didn't even have to learn them, because it occurred to me all of a sudden that I knew them. What I'm telling you now, it's because I'm dreaming, and no one will know."

"You're not dreaming, Cucoane Dominic," Nicodim insisted gently. "You're here with us, your friends; you're at the cafe. This is what we imagined would happen. When Cuconul Dominic comes to his senses, when he recovers from his amnesia, and returns, you'll see — he'll go straight to the Cafe Select!"

He began laughing again and looked at them all with a sudden intensity, as if he were afraid he would wake up at that very moment and lose all trace of them.

"But if I'm not dreaming, then you would know about Hiroshima and the hydrogen bomb and Neil Armstrong, the astronaut who landed and walked on the moon last summer, in July."

They were all silent, not daring to look at one another.

"So, that's what it was," the doctor spoke up at length. "You were mistaken for someone else."

He started to respond, but he was beginning to feel tired. He wiped his hand across his cheek several times.

"It's like the story of . . . of that Chinese philosopher. . . . You know who; I've told you several times."

"Which Chinese philosopher, Cucoane Dominic?" asked Vaian.

"I told you a little while ago," he replied irritably. "The name escapes me now. That story with the butterfly . . . Anyway, it's too long to repeat again."

He felt a strange fatigue throughout his body, and for a moment he was afraid he was going to faint. But maybe it would be better if I did, he said to himself. If I should faint, I'd wake up immediately.

"I've called for a sleigh to take you home, Domnu Matei," said someone. "Veta has a fire lit in the stove."

"I don't need any sleigh," he managed to say, rising from the table. "I'm going on foot. The next time the problem is raised, I'll know how to answer!"

"What problem, Domnu Matei?" Nicodim asked.

He started to reply, "The problem which worries all of us!"— but suddenly he felt all his teeth rattling, and embarrassed, furious, he clamped his jaws together tightly. Then he took several steps toward the exit. To his surprise, the others moved aside and allowed him to leave. He wanted to go back again and salute them all, raising his arm, but every movement exhausted him. Hesitantly, breathing heavily through his nostrils because he was holding his mouth tightly shut, he went out onto the street. The cold air revived him. I'm beginning to wake up, he told himself. When he thought no one would see him, he cupped his hand to his mouth and spat out his teeth, two or three at a time. He remembered vaguely, like some half-forgotten dream, that this same thing had happened to him once before: for some time he had been unable to speak because all of his teeth were loose. So, it's the same problem! he said to himself calmly, reconciled.

That night the doorman waited in vain for the return of the guest in Room 19. Then, when it began to snow, he telephoned the Cafe Select. He was told that a stranger, a gentleman, had come that evening and had gone directly to the back room. But after a little while, perhaps because the room was empty and poorly lighted, he had left without saying good evening, holding his right hand to his mouth.

In the morning, on strada Episcopiei, in front of house number 18, there was found, frozen, a stranger, very old, in an elegant suit and an expensive fur-lined overcoat. Both the overcoat and the other clothing were much too large for him, leaving no room for doubt that they were not his. Moreover, in the pocket of the jacket a billfold was found containing foreign currency and a Swiss passport bearing the name of Martin Audricourt, born in Honduras, November 18, 1939.

*Paris, November–December 1976*